BONDED BY LOYALTY

BONDED BY LOYALTY

Johnques Lupoe

BONDED BY LOYALTY

iUniverse books may be ordered through booksellers or by contacting:

iUniverse
1663 Liberty Drive
Bloomington, IN 47403
www.iuniverse.com
844-349-9409

Because of the dynamic nature of the Internet, any web addresses or links contained in this book may have changed since publication and may no longer be valid. The views expressed in this work are solely those of the author and do not necessarily reflect the views of the publisher, and the publisher hereby disclaims any responsibility for them.

Any people depicted in stock imagery provided by Getty Images are models, and such images are being used for illustrative purposes only. Certain stock imagery © Getty Images.

ISBN: 978-1-6632-3355-4 (sc)
ISBN: 978-1-6632-3354-7 (e)

Library of Congress Control Number: 2021925543

Print information available on the last page.

iUniverse rev. date: 12/09/2021

CHAPTER 1

Congo: BBL

"Bitch nigga don't move, you already know what time it is!"
Shouted Congo as he ran into the house. He waved the F.N around
the Room, eyes alert for the bull shit, making sure no one else was
in the room. That he could missed. As Congo walked over to the
goy, he made him get on the floor with his hand on top of his head.
Congo put zippy ties on the nigga to restrain him from moving as
he please. He ran through the small cozy two bedroom trap house,
tearing it up looking for the drugs and money he knew for a fact
that was there.

But he was looking over it. Congo went back into the living
room and sat the nigga up right, "Yo my nigga where that money at
hoh?" "Man you got the wrong man I swear." "Mother fucker I've
been watching you for the whole week, I know you got it up in here."
Man I don't have it, I swear I'm mine to five man."

Congo took the F-N and slapped the nigga across the head with
it and the gun went off by accident. The nigga told Congo hi real
name, birthday and social number. Congo couldn't help but grin a
little bit because he knew the nigga was tervified. So he asked him
again where the money and days was, but he didn't say a word. And
Congo getting mad because he didn't like to waste bullets or time.

Reggie didn't want to crack for shit. He knew he had to gone
head and shoot him for real this time, to let him know that he meant
business. Congo aimed the F.N at Reggie and out of nowhere a big
Red nigga with Deseeds busted in the house. He didn't ask no type

1

of questions as he started busting off shots. As he ran backwards trying to get behind a wall as he tried hard not to peel Reggie's cup back. But before Congo could make it behind the wall he had dropped the dread head.

"Enough playing in this mother fucker," growled Congo, Running back over to Reggie and shot him twice to make the nigga come one with the come on. Rigge and shot him twice to make the nigga come on with the come on. Rigge told him where the hole in the floor was and Congo wasted no time going to check it ovt. When everything checked out he took the duffle bag off his back and began to fill it up. Once he was done with that task, Congo turned to Reggie, told him thanks as he walked closer. Congo shot him once in the chest and once in the head, to make sure that baby was Rocked.

Congo came out of the house running full speed until he got to the hot box. As he got into the car he threw the duffle bag into the back seat, then started up the car. Smashing the gas like someone was after his ass, he made his way down the block. He was a smart individual and he always tried to stay a head of the cops and whoever he was gonna rob. Is minutes later Congo pulled up to the empty building where he parked his car, then switched Everything over. He wiped down the bot box and double checked to make sure it was clean as a dog bone. Congo never left anything behind if possible it was a rule.

He climbed into an all-black Vic and head home. Doring the drive Congo reached up under his seat and pulled out his ringing cell phone.

"Yo what's up fool" He answered, (caller ID read Gig T)

"Where you at bruh?" question Big T "Shidd, I'm on the way home, why, what you got going on?" "I got a play for some guns later tonight" "O.K Do I knew to call up Decatver Head to get us a car?" "I already got one, that's who I Just left seeing" "Then say no move, Just call me when you pull up" he told him, hanging up.

Congo pulled up at the condo but he noticed wasn't nobody at the apartment. "Dama where them nigga at when you need them" thought Congo, unbuckling the front door and gong inside with his stuff in tow. He locked the door behind him then went straight to his room. Congo threw the duffle bag of Goods on the bed, then pulled off all his guns. "Shit sometimes I feel like I love my guns more than this fucking money out here." He thought to himself, as he kid all his guns on the floor. Than knelt down to clean each one.

When he counted them he noticed no was missing. A .40 call Desert Eagle to be exact. Congo had to think.

What happen to it before he called Gutta and Season, bugging out to see if they had his staap. But the it hit him, he sold it to one of Gutta's friends the other day. He put all his guns in the chest left, it unlock but shid it all into the walking closet. It was itme to count his money.

20 bands, two pounds of weed and a large zip-loc bag full of ex-pills he refused to count up. Congo smiled to himself then said not bad out loud. He thought it would have been more but he was cool with the shit he came up on. He broke the money down to make sure everybody had some. 4 bands and both pounds of weed went to Season's Room. Then he took 4 bands and the zip-loc bag of pills to Guttg's bed Room. And as he was going back to his own bed room to get the 5 bands for the safe, he heard the front door open down stars.

3

"Yo, who dat?" "It's me Cherry" "Oh, where that nigga Gutta at, huh?" Coming in behind me now."

Congo grabbed the money and took it to their safe. That was their everything money, if they was short on rent, bills or bond money. Once that was all saved and done Congo went back to his bed room to put his money in his own safe.

Gutta: BbL

"Say Cherry,"

"Yea, daddy," "You know I got to see what you look like in all of them little outfits, before you hit the track tonight." Daddy you just trying to work your way in on some of this pussy before I go out.

"Bitch I ain't gotta work my way into shit I got control of, I just want to make gone you look real good and sluttie for tonight."

Gutta followed Cherry up stairs to their bedroom to put their stuff up. While Cherry went through her shopping bag, Gutta noticed a stack of money and zip-loc bag of pills posted up on his pillow. He smiled walking out his room going to see his boy." Say Congo!!!"

"Yo, bruh" "Where you at in this motherfucker?" "My room, why, what's up?' Gutta walked down the short ball to Congo room, and found him on the floor doing push-ups. "Man come on with all that swell nigga shit, I need your pants Jacket and boots, Terminator face ass nigga." "Bruh you know I gotta stay in shape especially playing around with them guns and shit, beside this how I stay a step ahead." "Well finish dong you; I just came to say thanks." Thanks for what? Asked Congo with a confused look plaster on his face. "The stuff you put on my pillow." "Oh, nigga you act like that's something we just started doing for each other, You know we

4

eat together around here" "Nigga I'd be at the track tonight if ya'll need me, Season been M.I.A all day."

Congo got up, grabbed his stuff then headed to the shower. "You know bruh do his best when he's out there hustling. But check this Gutta I should have some new toys later tonight."

he said as he shut the bathroom door. Gutta walked back to his room and Cherry was standing there smiling with a new outfit on. As he stepped into the room closing the door behind him, she turned around to show off the body fitting dress that barley could contain her whole ass. He sat on the foot of the bed to watch his Bottom Bitch model back and forth in all the outfits until he picked out the best one for the night.

CHAPTER 2

Congo: BBL

"Yo" answered Congo on the second ring

"Come on, I'm outside" Replied Big T, before hanging up

Congo Raced down the stairs and shot out the front door. He jumped into the suv with Big T, Congo checked out the hot box while they pulled off. It was a new Dodge Durango, all black and chrome out. "Man where you get this at, cause this ain't Deavtar Head M.O right here? Questioned Congo Big T didn't even say he just smiled and kept driving. Two hours later they had pulled up on the pawn shop that sat in the middle of nowhere, almost.

The fucking country side was weird like that in Georgia Big T parked the Suv by the woods and they jumped out Ready. Grabbing the sledge hammers and a pars of wire cutters out the hatch trunk, then ran across the street.

Congo handed Big T both sledge hammers and took the wife cutters, to kill the alarm system, then both camera cords. About time he went over to the main spot, Big T had already started trying to break dawn the wall. They took turns hitting the wall, until they made a big enough man-hole for them both.

The both of them ran around collecting hand guns and assault ruffles, sitting them all by the hole in the wall. Congo told Big T to go ahead and get the suv while he checked for a business safe. Big T went through the hole asap and saw a cop car drive by not really paying attention. He sealed the wall slowly staying in the shoulders, then ran to the Durango. Meanwhile Congo had begun his search, plus he loaded the guns and assault fuels into army duffle bags he found. Then set each boy out the hole. He did one last sweep through the pawn shop to make sure they had everything they needed or wanted.

While he was doing his sweep he found a miniature safe down by the camera recording box. Congo knew that it had to be a safe somewhere in there. He just over looked it the first time around. He grabbed the tape and then the safe, Running back to the manhole. Bout time he got there Big T was just backing up to the hole. Congo threw the safe and tape outside, before climbing out the hole. "Come on broh open he trunk up, you suppose to been halfway done loading this shit up by now," stressed Congo. Big T popped the hatch tank then jumped out the SUV door.

Leaving it wide open to help Congo put the bags on the inside, as soon as they put the last bag in the trunk and closed it, as the cop car was driving back around.

They hurried up and jumped into the SUV, hoping the cops didn't see them yet. As the cop car passed by the driver was smoking on a cigarette. Gig T slowly pulled off leaving the parking lot all normal. "That's why it took me so long" Expressed Big T "Fucking Country ass Cops" breath out Congo Not even five minutes into their drive down the long deserted Road the police pulled behind them, The same Cop car, Big T didn't even give them a chance to hit the lights. He hit the gas and didn't look back. Congo loved it when they got into high speed chases, because Big T always made the news and got away with it.

Congo was good at driving too but not like Big T, it didn't matter what kind of car he was in, just as long as it had a little speed to it. Big T got on the express way and sat up in his seat and it was like he became one with the Road. He took them all around 285 then got onto, 75 South then got off the Exit and took the back streets in and out of hoods until he lost the Cops. "Bet they stupid ass wish they had move back up." Joked Congo. Big T drove to his apartment complex off of camp Crack.

his front door. Soon as he got it open he waved at Congo to start bringing the bags inside. Congo got out the SUV and swung the hatch trunk opened. Grabbing two of the heavy bags and started Running for the door. Before he got even half why he got Big T Big ass to come help him out. The bag of guns felt more heavier than they usually did to Congo.

Big T took his ass into the apartment, Congo on the other hand dropped his bag right at the door, then went back to the Dodge Durango. He got the bag of bullets, safe and taps out next, Ran back to the apartment. Big T had already laid all of the guns and Rifles out on the floor, so they could pick what they rest up. Once they spitted all the guns and assault Rifles up they broke into the safe.

The only thing in it was a small back bag and a stack of cash. Big T grabbed the bag asap and opened it up, he laughed because it was full of dimes as he showed Congo what it was, Congo kept counting up the last of the money. It was only for bands. He spitted it up and put his half in his pocket, then told Big I to take him home. "Peaches!!!" yelled at Big T "Yes, baby!" She yelled back "Look I'm about to take Congo back home, so just keep an eye on things, You hear me?" "Okay baby and I aint deaf, dumb or blind, so you hurry up back home cause I've been missing you a lot today." Big T grabbed his car keys and headed for the door. "Yo Peaches, when you gonna hook me up with your sister!? Congo asked "Congo you not ready for my sister, she's a good girl like me" Responded Peaches giggling. "I know that's what I need, I need a good girl in my life," "Boy, I'll see what I can do for you." "Baby gone head and make that call for Congo, that way you'll be busy until I get back" Stated Big T. They left out headed towards Congo's spot.

Peaches: BBL

The phone rang eight times before Peaches got an answer.

"Hello?" "Coco girl guess who wants to talk to you, all of a sudden?"

"Who? And it better not be no lame or one of T's dusty home boys."

"Oh well, I'd tell him I tried then, bye sis,"

"Hold up Peaches, which one of his friends it was, Tim?

"Bad guess, Ew" "Who then? Dee, Black, Derives, Big G?"

"No all of them are bad Candidates and Girl you will be here all night trying to name the boys in my babies circle. It's Congo"

"Congo, Congo that drive that Black Crown vic?"

"Yes, girl that boy feeling you, he's been asking me about you a few times but I ain't think you would talk to him"

"Girl that boy is Fine, with all capital letters, is he around you now sis?"

"Nope, him and I just left out, they just got off work as my baby T would say" "Well you need to give Congo my number or set something up so we can hang out one night."

"Okay, I see I gots to do all the dirty work to get this boat Rocking, anyway love you girl but let me get off this phone, I'm trying to surprise my big baby when he get back in."

"Girl you are so nasty, nobody wants to actually know what it looks like to do it with Debo off Friday."

"Girl don't be hating, I just know how to keep a good man like Tari around, I let him make his money and have fun in the streets and I take care of home and he take care of me in return."

"Um, okay, well, just don't forget to make that happen for me, love you sis bye, I think you made me sick to my stomach"

"Whatever you little brat."

As big T and Congo pulled up at the Condo, Season was sitting on the hood of his car smoking a blunt. Congo gave Big T some dap, grabbed his bag out the trunk when he jumped out the car. And soon as he shut the trunk Big T drove off, hitting the horn twice like a fucking taxi cab driver. Congo gave Season some dap, no words was exchanged as they both sat on the hood finishing up the blunt. Both in their own thoughts and in turned with their surrounding as they in held the blunt of gangster-mid.

CHAPTER 3

Season: BBL

This morning Season still woke up Pretty early, but that was because of the vibration of his cell phone wouldn't let him sleep. He Rolled over fumbling around until he found it in the bed and answered it.

"Who dis?"

"Shawty I need two or's"

"Alright but who is dis first?"

"This man-man, Shawty"

"Alright, bacet me at the spot," Season said has he hung up.

Season got out of bed and got ready, then hit the streets with a new found energy. He hated old hated old school cars but that didn't stop him from taking Gutta's Cadillac, so he would be low-key. 30 minutes had went by before Season pulled up at the spot. A fast food joint, a pop eyes to be exact. He flashed his lights to let Man-Man know it was him, Man-Man walked to the Car and got in.

"Damn shawty, what's that you smoking on?"

"Here gone ahead and hit and tell me what you think of it yourself"

Man-Man hit the blunt hard as he cold, and started coughing ASAP. Season took the blunt back and began hitting it himself. After he hit it a few more times he let Man-Man know that it was sale and the price was a little bit higher.

"Shawty what type of weed is that? Questioned a red-eyed Man-Man

"It's something called girl scout, a dro type," explained Season
"How much it's going for shawty?"

"$550.00 an oz, but that just for you, I'm knocking off $150 really $200"

"Damn shawty that shit high but here rou go," cheesed Man-Man peeling the money off his bankroll. Seaso gave him the two oz's and the rest of the blunt as a bonus. Soon as Man-Man got out the car Season pulled off going about his business at hand. He picked up his cell phone to call back all of his missed call, to let everyone know that he was up and on the move.

Congo: BBL

Later that day at the condo Congo and Gutta was trying to put together a plan to hit up Myrtle Beach for Spring Baling, plus this was the one time where they really liked to put on. They was trying to figure out what kind of cars they was going to get and what they was going to do it.

"Daddy are you busy?" cherry yelled down stairs.

"I'm always busy in my line of work, but what's up?"

"I need you to talk me to meet this girl, she say she wants to work for your stable."

"Let's go; why you playing and shit when its new money on the hook" He told cherry. Then to Congo "we'd finish this later, I got to cheek this ho out real quick."

"Bruh I already known your M/o, Hell I gotta check on some things anyway myself" He went out to the car and as he got into the car his phone went off.

"Yo what it do?"

"Bruh Bruh this Tony, what you got news for me?"

12

"It depends on what you looking for, so I can grab it before I leave the house."

"I need a few hand guns and a choppa, Bruh Bruh."

"Ok I got ya, just meet me at our same spot on the east side." Then he hang up.

Congo Ran back in the house and went Right to his bedroom to pull out his straps. He got four hand guns and two Assault Rifles, putting them in his personal old army duffle bag. Congo ran back down the stairs and shot by Gotta and Cherry, who was also going out the door. As he loaded up his trunk Gutta and cherry finally came at the apartment looking like money. Congo got into the car then pulled off, as he drove off he hit the horn two times.

Gutta: BBL

"Cherry this Ho better be at least cute."

"She's more than cute daddy and her name is Tweely"

"Bitch you getting smart with me?!"

"No daddy"

Gutta smacked Cherry on her ass, watching it shake like jelleo, before she sat down in the car. "Season always hot boxing my shit," Gutta thought out loud climbing behind the wheel.

"Where do she stay at cherry."

"She's on the Westside over there by the job care, daddy."

Gutta hit the highway and opened up the engine. He wanted to really see what it drove like, because Season drove it when he dressed super clean to impress. he farther he made it down the highway, the more he started to respect the Q-45. It was a nice car but Gotta was a cadillac stunter. Gutta got to the Westside in no time, he drove

13

up to Tweety's crib and Cherry called her to come out. Gutta and Cherry got out the car and cleaned up against the hood.

It was like a Cartoon the way Gutta eyes lit up with Dollar signs as Tweety came at her house. She walked down the stairs.

and it was like the Sun was shining on her with hair blowing in the wind. Tweety walked to the car and stopped in front of Gutta and cherry smiled. Gutta graspped her by the hand and spun her around to check out his new product. Tweety was standing at about 5'7, pea can brown skinny sandy brown hair, with hazel light brown eyes and her ass looked like it was about 47 inches, with no stomach.

"You like what you see baby?"

"yeah it'll do, I just hope you're not a lazy fuck, with a body like that"

"No I like to work, so when do you want to start me baby?"

"Baby I'm not talking about being lazy like that, I'm talking about your sex game"

"Oh, baby I'm real good in bed do you want to try me out?"

"Bitch you aint did nothing in my eyes that's so great for me to hit you off ripe, so bitch you better stay in your place."

"Oh umm, damn sorry baby"

"It's daddy! check yourself before I check you, Now you Ho's get in the fucking car this pretty bitch done pissed me off."

Gutta went on mumbling about having dope dick and she had to do something good get it. Cherry looked at Tweety and shook her head cheesing flashing her Rose gold grille, As she climbed into the car herself. Twenty stood on the curb hands on her hips, with a puzzle look plastic on her face. Gutta started up the car then looked in the back seat to say something to Tweety and noticed she was still outside the car. He hopped out the car ran smoothly walked back around to where she was standing and quickly drew his hand back, pimp slapping her stupid ass to her knees.

"Bitch I didn't come way out here to play with you, Now get your ass in the damn car" Gutta said as he walked off without looking back. As he got in the car Gutta saw the back door shut before his's.

"Girl you my sister in law now, and rule number one is: do as you are told, simple as that," Chery looked back and explained to Tweety.

Gutta headed string to the Clinic that was right by high Tower train station. His first job was to make sure everything cheeked out with his new fine ass protect.

Congo: BBL

Congo finished up his business with Tony and heeded to meet Big T at the mall. Big T had peaches and CoCo with him. As he drove down the highway he called up season. "Yo bruh where you at?"

"I'm just riding around doing my usual" Answered Season

"Have you seen anything that looks like it would pay off good, yet?"

"Nah, not really but you know I'ma keep my eyes open for the exclusive"

"Ok, well what about one of your plays them?"

"Be easy, you know I need them,"

"Bruh you gonna get all the weed anyway"

"Just wait to one of them fuck up then I'm a give you the green loghh"

"Alight I'd see you later bruh, just keep keep me posted"

Congo parked the car and went inside the mall, soon as he walked in the saw Big T standing in the middle of the mall looking like a half giant. Coco and peaches was looking good, Congo pushed up and spoke to went one them gave Coco a huge friendly hug. Then they walked off, Congo let Coco stroll a few slick steps in front of him so he could check her out. The jeans she was wearing was like they been painted on her. Her Coco brown skin with long jet black hair and Hazel green eyes and a ass that could stop traffic had Congo messed up. He knew that he had to get her away from her sister and Big T, so he could see what she was like one on one.

Congo reach over and tapped Big T then gave him the signal that he was about to push on with Coco. He grabbed Coco by the hand and told her to come with him. As they walked through the mall Congo picked her brain to see where her head was at. Congo thought to himself. "This the one "I'd give my all to?" As they passed by the polo store he saw a fit that he just had to have. He turned around to go into the Polo store to cop the outfit. When they came out him and Coco both had two bags full of Polo shirt.

Congo was known for rocking all of the hottest top designers names but Polo was his main squeeze. Coco and Congo walked through the mall looking for Big T and peaches, but whenever Congo felt like spoiling Coco he would take her inside a stove and let her get a fly as outfit. But he let her know right off top what this wouldn't be an everyday thing if she became his lady. But she would get treated like a Queen if she acted Right. They met back up with Big T and Peaches two hours later. He dropped Coco off and told her to call him later if she got freed up. Congo left the mall and headed back home with Coco on his mind as well as a good like to hit.

CHAPTER 4

Tweety: BBL

The next morning Season Came down stairs and noticed some one a sleep on the sofa. He went to get a better look but the person was up under a blanket. Season tapped on what he figured was the foot to see who it was. And Tweety came from up under the cover looking even early morning good. He started questioning her off the muscle to see what she was dong sleeping on his sofa.

30 minutes later Congo came bouncing down the stairs and saw season standing there getting slow head by a thick fine pretty girl. Congo knew she had to be a G-Frock because she was serving Season up in the living room waking into the picture himself. Congo whipped his man hood out and season made twenty bend over. Season got behind Tweet's pat round ass and started busting her of the long strong way. While she slurped Congo up nasty style. When Congo got right him and Season went ahead and switched up.

They went back and for that beating them guts up, to her riding and sucking them up, to laying her back on her back. Tweety kept them on the verge of an orgasm but they would pull away from her to keep their control rate up. Congo and season tag teamed her fine ass for about 45 minutes, good heated inteass xxx Rated fun before Gutta came down stairs. He smiled flashing his whole grill damn near, cause season and Congo was always wilding out when they got a hold to a G-Freak.

The closer her got to the action Gutta realized that it was his new ho Tweety. He had forgot that she even stayed over last night.

17

He stepped in the living room, seeing how Congo and Season was tearing her ass up all he could say was "Bitch you know you dove fucked up right?!" Tweety popped Congo's dick out her mouth with the loud sound effects echoed through out the living room. She looked at her pimp with pleading eyes and moaned out "I'm sorry daddy, I thought you sent them"

Season was still hitting that wet while she was trying to talk her ass out of trouble. Congo was slanging his dick across her pretty face until she grabbed it in a tight grip. Gutta looked at Tweety and told her "Bitch make that shit quick and get yo hot ass up stairs." Gutta made his way to the stairs than told Tweety, "If I got to come back down here and get you I'm put my foot up yo ass, do I make myself clear?" "Crystal clear daddy."

Then she went to work on Congo making him hard again while she threw that wet-wet back on season. Tweety pussy was so good and wet to the point that Season cold barly handle it. Tweety knew her ass was going to pay for it later on tonight. She could still see her pimp daddy Gutta slick crazy ass fussing to himself about how she had the nerve to disrespect his pipmpin. As for his two Roommates was con corn they both just up and let her take all the heat. And she told herself if she ended up getting her ass whooped over this ordeal then she was going to curse both of them niggas out.

Gutta: BBL

As he got to his bedroom again Cherry was just getting up but she could tell something was wrong. She climbed out of bed ass naked and strolled over and hugged up on Gutta and asked him what was wrong.

This bitch is chis respectful"

"That she do now daddy?"

"Season and Congo got her stupid ass stretched out down there for free."

"Daddy do you want me to go down and handle her ass for you?"

"Nah baby, daddy got a rude awaking for her dumb ass, she gone stroll the track to her feet got sore."

"I'm about to go get myself together then daddy." Cherry said as she lend in and kissed Gutta's lips before she walked off. Gutta got himself together in the process too.

Congo: BBL

Once they got finished Congo shot up to his bedroom to get his things and went to the shower. He saw Season break for the other bathroom and about time they came out, they could hear Gutta down stairs going in on Tweety. He was putting that ho in check, to let her know.

that she by no means ever fuck shit or move an inch until he said so. Congo called Big T while he was getting dressed to make sure they was still going to Florida to mala that drop. Big T told Congo that he was on his way over as they speak, and he had everything he was gone sale. Congo got off the phone on that note and finished getting dressed.

He took the cast of his guns down stairs and sat them by the door. Congo glanced into the living room out the corner of his eye and saw Gutta slapping Tweety around.

"Oh, Congo you and Season going to pay me too."

"Congo laughed and said "Alright bruh"

Because this wasn't the first time they done tricked Getta's out of that wet-wet when they stayed over.

Season: BBL

Season came down the steps humming a Gucci Mane song, but as he walked out the front door he yelled into the living room and told Gutta "Thanks for that early morning wake up service, Pimpin!"

Then went outside and lit his blunt up, as he chilled on the porch he thought to himself "Damn bitch your ass in big trouble now."

Gutta: BBL

Butta smacked Tweety back down to the ground then kicked her a few times before he told her to go upstairs and get herself together. The only real reason he beat her ass was because he had to go back down stairs and get her. "Cherry!" Yelled Gutta behind Tweety as she ran upstairs.

"Yes, daddy?" Answered cherry peeping over the stair well

"What you hiding for bitch, do I need to come up there and whoop yo ass to?"

"No, daddy" she responded quickly

"Get that bitch together and you better talk some sense to her before I kill her fine ass."

"I'd handle it from here daddy, come on Tweety"

Gutta grinned knowing that, that ass whooping would keep Tweety in line for a while. He made sure not to bruise her up, but he also let her ass know that he was holding back.

Congo: BBL

Congo loaded up his trunk, as he was shutting it he saw Big T coming around the corner. He went and started up his car, Big T pulled up bouncing around in his seat with the music up loud.

"Yo what you on this early bruh?"

"Shidd, bruh I'm just ready to ride out so lets go."

"Oh alight, well pop your trunk so I can get the guns out then"

Season from the porch started Rapping "Hot boys, Hot, Hot, Hot boys" Shaking his head Congo walked to the back of Big T's car and unloaded the guns. After they got loaded up Big T parked his car and they took off.

Gutta: BBL

Gutta came out the crib with Cherry and Tweety following close behind him. All three of them drop in some red dressed to impress the nosy eyes, then the hungry lustful minds.

"Ya'll ho's go get in the car" ordered Gutta

"Okay daddy, said Cherry leading Tweety to the Cadillac

"Season you need me to lock up or you going back in side?"

"I'm out too, but I'd back up cause I'm about to get on my grand and set a few Records."

"Yeah, me too, this bitch gots to make up form earlier, be cool and safe" said Gutta giving his boy some dap before walking off towards his car. Where his hog sat waiting like good little girls.

Season: BBL

Season just smiled at Gotta who climbed into the car and pulled off, lecturing his hos still. He hit the blunt a few more times, he didn't need nothing out the crib he could think of. So he locked the front door. "Now who got a fly car I can take for a quick spin?" He asked himself as he climbed in to the Q-45. The it hit him his uncle Bobby's new baby mom just coped cone of them Mercedes Benzes 550. And she drove her cars factory just like him, so Season called her up to see how she was doing.

Congo: BBL

Hours later Congo and Big T was arriving into Daytona bench flat where they always met up with their 305 boys. Congo and Big T never wanted to go all the way to Miami to handle business. Just in case something flaky jumped into the mix, they would have a better chance of getting away. He spotted his man, got out the car walking over to Great him. "What it do All?"

"Shidd you know me, just trying to make a living"

"So what you got for me this time."

"Well I got some mint- 14s, Mac-90's Glook 40 cals, AK-47s, SK-, Mac-ll Desert Eagles, 2-F-N's and Bersett so cal, oh yeah I almost forgot the .380 special."

"Damn that's what's up, ok well I only have 12,000.00"

"Ok so you want the usual, well let me get your stuff ready."

Congo walked back to the car with a brown sack and threw it on the front seat. Big T position his own 2 F-N's in quick draw reach before snatching up the money and counting it. Congo unloaded the trunk, Already thinking about his new collection of Art. Once he was finished Congo dapped 305 up and told him it was nice doing business with him as usual. As Congo got in the car and drove off he looked at Big T to make sure everything was straight. Big T just gave him the head nod like Yeah, nigga we good! Congo hit the gas on that gue and jumped back on highway as heading home.

Gutta: BBL

Meanwhile back in the city Gutta had Tweety and Cherry trying out this new spot he had found. It was dang some good numbers to, just having them two out there wasn't gone be enough eventually. Gutta knew that this was his official new spot when things got hot every where else. He just had to keep the spot on the low-low. If any other pimp got whipt of it, he'd have to run them off or go start to war with them. Four hours later and 10,850 show profit, Gutta loaded Cherry and Tweety up with a proud smile.

He was taking them to fishing up at a motel so they could represent him on the main track.

"Tweety"

"Yes, daddy"

"You did good, keep up the hustle to and daddy will keep smiling"

Tweety beamed in the back seat, she had rights to because she worked the hell out that new spot. Making money for her daddy was the only thing on her mind. "Cherry"

"Yes, daddy"

"Yes, daddy"

"Bitch you let the new ho at do you again and I'm gone put my foot in your ass" the catrn Gutta

"Sorry daddy it want happen again I swear" Pouted Cherry shooting Tweety a quick glance and winded at her when Gutta was making a turn. Cherry let Tweety catch the last trick when Gutta called them in. So Tweety was able to make that extra $50 and only God knew she needed it, how she been keeping their daddy on edge from jump street.

"Thank you" Mouthed off Tweety silently

"We're sister-N-laws now, I got your back" Cherry Mouthed back

"Damn that's a nice piece right there" Pointed out Gutta, pulling into Church's chicken parking lot. The girl was a short petite, big tits bubble butt almost while in completion orange headed cuts little piece for real. He pulled alone side the girl window down and asked "You look like your name is Ice-cream miss lady, so what's your flavor?"

The girl burst out laughing because the come out line was corny.

"What you see is what you get pretty much with me" She had told him

"Oh shit her teeth is fucked up, for real" whispered Cherry

"How tall are you if you don't mind me asking?"

"I'm five foot even."

"I'm Gutta, this Cherry and back there is Tweety"

"Hey, everybody my name is Joyce"

"I'm call you Ice-cream because I know you going to taste good"

Joyce eyes coiden in shock surprised and she was blushing hard. Within 15 minutes time spin fiesta found out she was a New York born and raised black/Irish make, she wanted to have fun and lately she'd been bored to death of Atlanta. But once she accepted Gutta's invitation for a ride whole life was about to change.

Season: BBL

It had done got super late for his taste bid, and Season was getting a fresh outfit together so he could go at to Central Station. Duheem dirlnt have a party going on this weekend, so he had to hit the club since instead. Congo and Gutta pulled up at the same time. Gongo and Big T got out the car with some College park shoe store bay so Gutta looked at them and it was like they was all on the same page. Going out tonight plus Gutta had another bad bitch with a jacked up grill, that he called Ice-cream alone for the party. He pulled Gutta off to the side about the girl.

Shawty and ass for days on that little ass frame of hers, whats her story pimping?"

"Black and Irish Taylor made, Orange hair and hips is that Irish shit" and her father side of the family got a fat ass"

"Hold up you talking about all the bitches Right?"

"She say 91% of the family that including the niggas to "burst out laughing Gutta

"Damn that's fucked up for real" Chucked Season

Gutta gave him a little more of the girl back ground history, the fact was she was only 16 of age. Season knew nine times out of ten that his boy Gutta was gone put a baby in Ice-cream, probably Tweety too.

Cherry: BBL

In the hot shower Cherry goaped up the ray real good, staring at Tweety who was up under the shower head, she slowly washed the other girl with tender care. As bottom bitch she had to gain second control over every ho in Gutta's stable. Cherry control came from one on one trust that bonded two women. Sexing them was cherry lock-hold specialty. So after the both were clean she gave Tweety a sample of her pit-bull treatment.

Cherry cupped Tweety's chain tenderly and moved her lips towards the other girls, and gently kissed her. Tweety didn't resist, so cherry knew right then it wasn't her first time with another woman. They kissed passionately while fondling's each other until it got intense.

"Put your left leg over my shoulder" order cherry squatting directly in front of the other girl. Tweety really got deep into it, when Cherry slid her tongue down her wet-wet and wrapped her lips around the clit Cherry moaned out sucking on Tweety's clit like a pacifier. They was able to get a good heated 20 minutes in giving or taking before Gutta busted into the bath room.

"Yall bitches ain't got all day to play around in there, Cherry kiss that sweet pussy for daddy."

"Okay daddy" giggled Cherry before kissing Tweety's hot spot.

Tweety giggled too, staring back into Gutta's eyes until he left out leaving the bath room door open. Even though she didn't fully understand her new life style, Tweety couldn't help but respect his pimping.

CHAPTER 5

Congo: BBL

The club music blasted throughout the bouncing off every wall to give it that quaking sensation feeling. Gutta, Cherry, Tweety and Ice-cream al went straight to the V.I.P section. While Season and Congo walked the floor to see if they could come up on some soft legs, Fat ass, tiny waist nice tits and decent face. Just something a hood nigga could relate too…

Congo bumped into Big T and Peaches while he was scanning through the thick crowd. "I see you made it" Smiled Congo giving him some dap.

"Yeah, lil bruh we been here for about ten minutes and yo girl here somewhere"

"Oh, so you brought Coco with you, huh!?"

"Nah, they was already planning to come, I drove my own car"

"Ight that's what sup, well we up in V.I.P so tell the girls to gone up"

"Alright" responded Big T, while he scooped out a few niggas.

Congo pushed off and the whole time he was walking in and out the crowds he was looking for alike to hit straight after the club. Something in he heat of the moment if possible. He bumped back into Big T an hour later dancing with peaches and Coco.

Congo grabbed Coco by the hand and spinned her around. Before she could get a protesting word out her mouth she realized that it was Congo. She gave him a huge smile and a huge hug with a drawn out kiss on the cheek. The DJ had changed the song and it was an old song from Twister Make that ass roll like some 24". Coco turned around and started shaking and grinding her ass all up on Congo. Song after song the D, played nothing but hits that would make a chick turn the fuck up and got loose with it.

Coco didn't stop dancing loving how Congo was brick hard and pressed against her butt. She glanced back over her shoulder, smiling while blowing him a kiss. Congo stopped Coco and grabbed her by the hand and took her back to the V.I.P section booth. He sat down far away from the others after interdicting everyone every one. Coco straddle his lap, biting her bottom lip, and Congo palmed her ass.

"When are you planning on making me your girl, huh?" She questioned

"Baby are you sure you are even ready to be my lady?"

"Why wouldn't I be Congo?"

"Cause I live a crazy life style, matter of fact hold on a second to that thought baby."

Congo lifted Coco up, sitting her to the side and left out the U.I.P in a hurry. He had spotted a nigga with white + yellow diamond necklace, earrings and a bracelet to match. Congo knew he had to have that nigga and before he could get on the dance floor good enough Big T had done pushed up on him. "Lil bruh its a nigga in here putting on big time "Explained Big T with hungry in his eyes.

"Yeah, I know, that's why I just came down on the floor" Chased Congo flashing his pull out top and bottom designer cut 18k gold grille.

"We got to have that nigga fronting ass."

"You already know, we going to eat that kid, so just keep your eyes open Big T and Congo split back up and kept their eyes on the prize. Congo somehow made it close enough so he could get a real good look at the nigga face and jewelz. The necklace looked liked it coasted about 30 to 40 g's, but he really couldn't tell right off back. Because he didn't know what karat cuts that tell right off back. Because he didn't know what karat cuts the diamonds where.

"Say silly Rabbit, can I have a Karat or two" thought Congo Smirking anxious to touch that boy.

Congo want back to the V.I.P to chill with Coco who he found putting because how he just up and left her. Gutta and Cherry was getting the other two girls, Ready to leave.

"We'd see you and Season back at the crib, Iron man"

"Ok, that's what sup. Just keep your phone close by you bruh"

"Sound about right, You be safe my nigga"

Gutta + Cherry always left the club sense early because they never wanted to be caught up in any of that bullshit that goes on after it closed. While Congo was making small talk in the both with Coco, two nice looking girls strolled by and spoke to him, Coco turned and looked at him like "Who are those hitches?" Congo couldn't do nothing but smile and told Coco "don't start that crazy mess". 15 minutes had done passed by and Big T was in and out the V.I.P tracking their prize down for the night. They had to make that money back up form buying all of them bottles of bubbles and Goose. Both of them made sure everybody had a good time when they walks with them but that was all part of their trick.

Gutta: BBL

Sence Cherry had found her a late night private date. Gutta lead Tweety by the hand to the ladies Room. And Tweety had in tow by the hand to the ladies Room. And Tweety had in tow by the hand ice-cream, Neither one knowing what was up. He found a empty stall in the middle and all three of them went inside of it and locked the door. Once inside Gutta told Tweety "turn around, bend over and hold that down for daddy baby" Giggling Tweety did as she was told, Ice cream behind the two giggling like a little school girl.

Gutta pulled his pants and boxer shorts down to his Knee's handed Ice-cream his Chrome walter ppk. 380 with the pearl red handles. He ripped open the red life style com don wrapper, Rolled it onto his man hood, before digging deep into Tweety wet guts.

"Aaaahhh, that...my....my oh daddy....that's my spot right there!" moaned out Tweety throwing it back on him.

"You gonna keep, daddy happy baby" grunted Gutta fighting the urge not to explode in the first 20 minutes.

"Yes, oh gawd-cried out Tweety daddy please don't stop!"

Another twenty had done passed and Tweety had caught wave of a double douse back to back orgasm. Ten minutes later Gutta pulled out and made her sit on the toilet seal. He pulled off the Condom and Tweety put that bomb ass head on Gutta until he netted all up in her mouth. When the three of them stepped out the stall it was over two dozen girls blushing, smiling and whispering. Walking the crowd of girls most of them spoke to him as he passed close by them.

Season: BBL

He had to slid out to his car three times already to re-up on 100 sacks of wed. While in the club all season ever sold was Dib's nothing short or nothing over. It was a slick low key hustle system he used to stay up under the radar.

"Boy let me get three for the $50" said pull over.

He didn't know pullover real name she was jet back "Dark Chocolate" 5'3 super thick out Ragouts donkey booty Miami chick.

Pull over knew her ass for days caught hustlers attention no matter where she went. She was some what cute, had 18k white gold slugs on either side of her two front tooth and same at the bottom. Plus a tongue ring to match both slugs and diamonds in her tongue Ring. Pull over also Rocked two diamond 18k white gold Necklace; three Rings, a bracelet, watch and earrings.

"How much all your jewellery coasted you, huh" Smiled Season as he checked out her ass.

"It ran me $3,050 and some change, why" checked Pullover

"And you short on my paper by $10"

"Boy don't start that party shit with me cause I'd shoot at on your ass."

"You act like you be swinging thought my crib, showing me and my brothers Crazy love with that fat ass, Now you need me" Season told her pulling out three Dub Sacks.

Season knew all the stories about pullover, Niggas claim that the wet-wet and mouth was point Dexter. This will be his day to get behind all that ass, just so he could see all the tricks she had in store. Ass control is what they say she had and that Huge mother fucker was super loose in them stretch pants she was rocking tonight.

Congo: BBL

When people with money saw them blowing money like that, they always pushed up and wanted to party with them. And they would party all night if needed be, Just so they could rob them later. Big T and Congo told Peaches and Coco to go ahead and leave, because the club was about to close and they had some business to handle. While they was leaving out Big T nothing that the prize kid was about to bounce as well. So him and Congo left right along with Peaches and Coco. Big T gave Peaches his key and told her to let Coco drive her car home.

Then he walked off to get in the car with Congo. They sat in the car waiting the kid to come out the club. Ten minutes alter the nigga came walking out the club. With a thick little chocolate chick with melon size fits. It was the game drunk groupie that tried to party with them. That was even better for Congo cause when it was all said and done he could put it off on her on her like she set everything up.

They watched the couple get into a red and white 94 Cadillac. Elder do, sitting up on chrome 22 inches spinners. As they pulled out the club parking lot Congo gave him a few minutes, then tailed behind them. They followed him back into east point, and this nigga must had God on his side because all the lights was getting frustrated cause he couldn't catch the nigga at no lights.

Out the blue Congo speeded up good enough so he could tap the bumper just right to make him stop. But trying not to mess up his own car. The nigga stopped in the middle of the road and Congo jumped out his car acting like he was drunk, walking towards the Cadillac driver door.

"Are man you alright?" Asked Congo in a slur

"Yeah Shawty I'm good, but you shouldn't be driving that messed up"

Yeah I know, I'm just trying to make it home"

"Well everything cool on my end what about you?"

"Nah everything aint good on my end"

"What? Shawty you need help?"

"Yeah, now that you asked

Congo bent over like he was about to throw up and the nigga walked closer to check on him. That's when Congo stood up pulling the desert Eagle off his hip.

"Bitch nigga this a stick up don't move!" Said Congo

Soon as Big T saw Congo pull the gun he got out the car running to the Eldaro to make sure ol girl wasn't calling the police. He pulled her drunk ass out the car and made her get on the ground next to ol boy. Big T went back to search the car while, Congo was stripping dude for everything he had on his person. All he left him in was his under wears and T-shirt and then did the chick the same way.

Big T ran back to the car with one back bag and one brown bag. Congo started backing up them ran to the car. As he shut the car door he slapped the gear in reverse and hit the gas hard. Once he felt like he was good enough down the road. Congo did a 360º in the middle of the street and put the gear in drive to haul ass. He watched Big T go through the bags to see what all they had in them. Them brown had 6 bands in it and the black one had two pounds of weed and 2 cookies of crack. Big T split up everything before he got dropped off.

As Congo was pulling off his cell phone went off "Hello"

"Baby you wasn't gonna come inside and at least kiss me goodnight"

"Hell I thought you was gone already"

"Well it's always tomorrow"

"So you telling me that you mine now?"

"Shoot baby I been yours and you aint even know it until now"

Congo talked to Coco his whole /ride home.

Gutta: BBL

He had Tweety, it was a total of 43 Ho's out clocking. At first Gutta walked up and down the track to make sure it was safe for his HO to do her thing. He pushed up on other pimps ho's who wasn't on the since selling them ex-pills at $25 a pop. A super ugly bad body Ho that went by the name "Yokk". She stood 5'6, peacan dusty brown, with a big ass head on her shoulders, bedroom eyes, wide nose, puffy cheek bones and a wide mouth. Yokk had droopy melon size tits, she wasn't pregnant, but you'd think she was at least seven mothers from labor.

Her ass was a 46½ inch juicy bubbly thing, connected to thunder thighs and bowlegs.

"So I ain't no money maker, in your book huh?" She questioned getting in his face. "Nah, you get major props on this track here, but on the real you need to tighten up body wise, then I'd consider you being a part of my stable"

"Oh yea that's right I forgot that you only want the best looking ones, but just so you know I make 3,150 night"

Gutta heard she made a real killing on the track only because she was out there all night. He didn't respond to her statement. But he did smack her on the ass, just as she her teeth about to stroll off.

"You wouldn't even know what to do with what's between my leg" she shouted from over her shoulder then look off.

Gutta watched that ass of her's until it climbed into a early 80's model Corvette vert. He saw that ho, who went by Bad love jumping out a late 60's model chervil e 55. Gutta pushed up on the Ho about the money she owed him ASAP.

"Ho you aint heard about Gutta yet?" He had a death grip on her arm. Nigga don't be grabbing me like I'm yours, let me go!" Bad love tried to Jerk away slap! Slap! Gotta pimp slapped her twice across the face. First a open palm followed by the back hand. "Where my mother fucking money"

Bad love put Gutta in the mind of Ruff Ryder EVE with cat green eyes. "You dead now let me go, nigga!"

"Bitch you go heart I'd give you that, but you gone pay me my money" Gutta pushed her up against the brick wall in the ally he caught her in, "Bitch I'm the wrong nigga to try that shit on". Bad love got nervous as hell, her ass just knew she was in trouble. He quickly got around to whipping out his blood. She stared at it as it grew its full size in lust horror.

"Oh you want some of this magic stick don't you Ho?"

He was slim, but was strap! Licking her dry lips shaking her head yes, she always thought Gutta was a cut as pimp. Rough around the edge but smooth with hsi actions. Gotta used both hands to pull up her blue jean skirt, No panties, the lifted her right up to cradle it in his left arm.

"Oh, hold...holdup, mmmm, we need a co...need a condom" she moaned out as he slowly penetrated her.

"Fuck a condom, you owe me Ho, Now take this dick back" grunted Gotta feeling how tight she was.

Three minutes in, Gutta grabbed Bad love by her neck nad continued to dig off into her kitty and enjoying his handy work.

"Aaaahh, shit...fuck me daddy, Aaahh daddy!" Bad love chanted as she rapidly moved her hips back and forth trying to let Gutta go deeper inside her, but she was damn near climbing up the wall using him as a stepping later. Two Ho's came down the ally to be nosy but Gutta threats Ran them off fast.

Pullover strolled through the ally crying from the operative of the track, she saw them and smacked her teeth then rolled her eyes at Gutta. She was beyond upset. Within 45 minutes Bad love had a orgasm and so did Gutta, who sleeted all inside of her. He put her leg down but her other one was still locked around him like a snake. Bad love knew she was dead as wrong for fucking another pimp, eypecially on the track with all these gossiping Ho's. Gutta pulled her halter top down, exposing her lacy green bra, then quickly pulked the folded money out of it before she could protest.

"What are you doing I just paid you Gotta"

"Double or nothing bitch." He shot back flipping through the bills nothing that it was all $100⁰⁰

"You gonna get me in trouble," she whined, fixing her clothes to normal.

"See you around Badlove, it was nice dong business with you bitch" he said, pulling up his pants then walking off still counting his new money.

"Fuck you Gutta!" called out Badlove as he got a descent distance. She didn't know if she would have to run from his crazy ass.

But she heard him bust out laughing all devilishly and that shit gave the chill in the low light dark ally. Back in the Cadillac Gutta asked Ice-cream was she hungry or anything. Shaking her head no." I still can't believe a pimp, I mean a real pimp" Ice-cream told him.

"Do that bother you?"

"No not really"

"The money is great as you can see for yourself, pussy is powerful in this land we just don't understand why. Me and my girls V.I.P things everywhere we go, take long trip Just because we got to much money on head. And we go shopping off the chain every Friday." Gutt told her.

CHAPTER 6

Congo: BBL

Within the next morning since Longo hated sleeping long he got up. He had three new messages on his phone call from Coco who really couldn't sleep at all. Congo listen to them as he got dressed, he know Coco really liked him. So he made plans to surprise her today, so they could hang at after he finished handling business. He left the crib and headed straight to Jimmy Carter Bud, to see hsi main man Jacob the Jewelor. It was time to get that cha-ching!

Season: BBL

Season got up and got Ready to start his day off Right, He Got dressed then woke up pullover and told her to help him break down and bag up the fresh pound. Congo drop it off in his Room this morning alone with a chuck of doper. Season just put the cookie into a sandwich bag. Pullover took a quick shower as he went over everything twice. Ten minutes later Season grabbed all of his work, told her ass to come on, because he was ready to hit the streets.

All it took was for one person to know that he was up and moving around. And now his cell phone wouldn't stop ringing. Season Rolled from the south side, to the eastside back to the Westside making plays but working Pullover. Time had flew by and the only thing he ain't sold yet was that stinky ass cookie. Season made a run back to the crib to stash money and grab some more work, because he had sold everything they had broke down early. As he was walking into the condo Cherry was on her why out.

"Season are you still using my car? Asked Cherry eyeing pullover

"Yeah, sis I'm about done for the day, I just need like one or two hours"

"Ok well take your time and Gutta up stairs in the Room if you need him."

Season looked at Cherry with a puzzled look on his face as she left in a hurry. Because she never left the house without Gutta like that. He ran up stairs to re-up after telling pullover to chill on the sofa.

"You seen Cherry down stairs?"

"You seen Cherry down stairs?"

"Yea she was leaving out as I came in, why what's up?

"Hell if I would have known you coming back at this time, I would have told her to trick that nigga New York Black out of some weed for you."

"You know we need all we can get, you slipped then pin pin."

"I'm about to call her now, to see if she answer."

Gutta went down stairs to get Season Keys off the table so he can pick up his other ho's, to put them to work early. Season found Gutta in the living Room holding at Pullover, so he told her to ride out with Gutta instead. As they left the crib Congo was passing by them heading home. They all hit the horns.

Congo: BBL

Congo parked the crown Vic, then him and Coco went into the apartment. He took Coco up to his bedroom to welcome her in as being his lady. Congo sat Coco on the bed then pulled out the money that he had done got for the jewellery. All together it was about $45 bands. He broke the money down into two stacks and then gave Coco the extra grand. She was excited because Coco never had a man that was making as much money as Congo. And was willing to share it.

Congo wrapped Big T money up and sat it on the dresser next to his stack. Then walked over to Coco and laid her back on the bed. He started kissing her from head to feet while he was taking off her clothes. Then began kissing on her inner things as he worked his way up to her kitty, and begun licking and sucking on her clit while he fingered he with one hand. Coco let out a soft Moan as she got more in the mood. Congo pulled her to the edge of the bed then placed himself inside of her. Going from slow to fast Congo was giving her just a sample of what's to come.

Gutta: BBL

Him and pullover talked all the way to the hotel he left Tweety and Ice cream at. At the track Pullover put in work alone side of Tweety. Ice-cream still wasn't ready so he made her hold his money, as he hit the curb to shoot dice with the over pimps. Ten minutes into the crap game one of the hoe's who caught him in the ally last night, spoke to Gutta flirtatiously and got her dumb ass smacked up by her pimp Rat.

"I'm Riding with Gutta" a old pimp named smooth Cash around "Who don't like us" question Gutta woven money around.

"I don't like you, for $500" Rat told him, dropping money at his feet.

Gutta counted out $500 then tossed it on top of Rat's money knowing the pimp felt some type of way. He didn't know word was already out about him taking Bad love up through there. Gutta was hot Rollin every time up his money so did Smooth Cosh who was the only other pimp side betting with him.

"Ya'll get on ya'll pimping, bets went from $50 to $500 now it's $10, my ho's clocking dough out this mother fucker. Don't let me find out that a pimp name Gutta winning all around the bored, I'd never take my foot off ya'll niggas neck" boasted Gutta, betting the eleven pimps $10 each.

For good drops later Gotta broke eight of the pimps then fell himself. Another pimp that went by shawty Jones got on the dice hit back to back then went out losing more then he won. Every pimp on the block eyes was on that pimp True love GS bubble Cherry, as it sped towards them. All the other pimp Jumped out the way except Gutta. When the caprice came onto the curb at full speed, True love came to a screeching halt.

A good foot directly in front of Gutta give or take.

"Nigga where my money at, my trap aint free"

"Pimping check yourself like you check your ho's out there, the tap consist of hustlers, so if you not fit to meet the correct profile get your ass out the way, my time or game ain't free, therefore when you messed up my crap game you owe me $11,000, $9,000 for time and 6,000 for my game nigga do you got that? Gutta was dead ass serious too pulling out his cell phone and text Congo

Congo: BBL

He flipped her over and pulled her ass closer to him, then started stroking her insides while he gripped and smacked her on the ass. Congo grabbed his cell phone off the pillow, it was going off, so he went ahead and answered it to see what season wanted or needed,

Gutta and season was the only two that had their own Ring tone for his phone.

Still stroking in a slow circular motion, watching Coco bite back her moans.

What's up bruh this better be important?"

"Bruh I need your help this nigga just robbed me!"

"What" on the Westside, I've been following this nigga and his stupid ass don't even know it."

"Tight give me a second I'm on the way."

Congo hung up and tossed the phone on the bed then told Coco he was very sorry for what he was about to do. But he was going to make it up to her later. He grabbed her by her hips and begun pounding into her kitty cat from the back fast and harder. Coco dropped her head into the pillow he had the cell phone on the first time. In less than ten minutes, she told him she was Cumming. He went even harder in the paint just to leave his mark. Bouncing up against her corner until he was netting Next.

Then Congo told her to put her clothes on cause they had to go. Season was in a fucked up situation and needed him ASAP. As she put his gear on Congo looked in the closet to see which gun he needed to take. He grabbed the F-H and the stack of money that went to Big T, then headed for the bedroom door. Coco was sitting on the bed looking lost because Congo her new man changed within seconds.

At first he was making good love to her, then the next minute he was glutting her out which excited her. Now watching him strap with a gun kinds scared her out her with. And she didn't know what to think or do after she got dressed. But when Congo turned around at the door and told her to come on, Coo quickly ran at the room behind him. Once they got into the car, Congo explain to her, what all he wanted her to do when they met up with Season.

Then Congo called Big T telling him that he was sending Coco over there in his car, with his half of the Jewellery money. Hanging up then he called Season back to make sure he was still on the Westside. Congo made his was to Simpson Rd where he met his bruh at the BP gas-station. He pulled up next to Season's car and got out taking the F-H and putting it in the car with Season. He Ran back to his car, passenger side and gave Coco a kiss. Then told her that he would call her later.

Congo jumped in the car with Season and they drove off. While they were headed back to the spot where Season got Robbed, Congo asked what happen and also wanted to know where was Season's gun at? Season explained everything to him then shown him what apartment the nigga Ran into. It was one thing that Congo hated more then he hated not having money, and it was for some One to fuck with his friends or family. Gutta, season and Big T was all the really had when it boiled down to it.

Congo asked Season one more question, he wanted to know that the nigga looked like, so he could make sure he got the right target the first around. Season told Congo what he wanted to know, but turned Right around and told him that he was going with him. Shit was personal in Season eyes. As they got out the car Congo looked at Season and told him if anything got out of hand, to get the hell out and wait somewhere safe for him to call.

They walked up to the apartment door and Congo knocked on it, after telling his bruh to step to the side.

"Who is it?"

"Yung, is Candy home?"

The door open up and the nigga came half way out "There's no Candy that stay here little nigga."

Congo kicked the nigga into the front door as he pulled the F-H from behind his back. The nigga tumbled to the floor but got back up fast as fuck. Congo and Season took off into the apartment wide open. He snatched the nigga up by his collar and pulled him back before he could take off running down the hall. Congo placed the F-H in the nigga's face, Season closed the front door then Ran over nad slapped the hell out of him. And two teeth came out the nigga's mouth. The gun had went off and the bullet went flying through the walls of the apartment. The nigga asked them what did they want with him because he didn't have money.

"Where my crack you stoke out my car punk?"

"I...I put it in the bedroom"

Season ran to the bedroom looking for his shit, he found it under the bed on a plate. The nigga had started chopping it up to get him a hit. Sweeping all the crack back into the bag season smiling. Congo let the crack head up so they could leave up Gutta there. Season walked by and acted like he was about to slap the nigga again. The crack head folded up and both Congo and Season burst out laughing. Congo Kicked him in his ass bone, then ran out the apartment headed to the car.

The crack head came out behind them two minutes later shooting at them. Congo and Season returned fire ducking behind a car. The crack head Ran out of bullets first, so they opened fire while running to their car. They climbed in the car and hauled ass.

Cherry: BBL

She didn't get to Gutta's text a few hours later. Gutta wanted her to juice New York Black out of some weed. Cherry paraded around the hotel room in her birthday suit, champagne glass full of bubbles filled to the brim. New York Black sat on the edge of the bed with the bottle in his hand, cell phone on the other talking to his complaining wife.

"Yo Shorty we're not about to go through this right now, I'm not handling business, One" then hung up, taking a swing of bobbles, sitting his phone on the bed.

"Baby, I'm not trying to get all up in your business but...." New York Black cut her off on some real aggressive shaft.

"Than don't your cause I ain't leaving my wife for no bitch"

"I said your business, not your bitch, which I could care less about nigga!" She snapped all nasty

"Yo so what are you saying?"

I'm saying if you want a A-1 local middle man, I got some one for you, this nigga quitted and well respected in this city for real that if your serious Black" She explained.

"Say word and you trust kid like that?"

"I trust hustling skills, baby" answered Cherry straddling his lap

Season: BBL

On the highway Season got cherry's text and told Congo about his new plug. Him and Congo was in the middle of talking about their trip coming up soon. Season already knew his two partners were planning on stunting hard on them folks in Myrtle Beach.

Himself on the other hand was going to rent a fly ass car or sun call it a wrap.

"So what about our living arrangements again?"

"I got a friend whose Aunt stay down there, she say for $30,000 we can rent out the penthouse in the hotel she's Assistant Manager at, that $10,000 each"

"Yeah, one never know who they're running with these days and my mentor told me to keep checking for signs, and so far passing all the check points congo" teased Season.

"That de ass nigga mister Jay really firing your brain Season"

"some of the shit Mister Jay being saying is on point, but after an hour or so the nigga ol ass start laying for no reason, the when you confront him he say lies are more valuable than the truth in most cases".

"I caught his ol ass lying one day and told, him to stop that shit, His ol ass told me that lying is Healthy stress reliever for the brain."

Season and Congo both burst out laughing at the expense of Mister Jay crazy ass. Mr. Jay was a street Hustler to the bone but a Jack of all trades to the Core. Every time Season wanted to know how to move a sort way all he did was track down me. Jay for the inside, behind the sence 4.4.1.

Congo: BBL

He felt his cell phone buzz in his pocket, indicating a text message was in his inbox. Congo Just shook his head

Once he had read the text Gutta sent. "Track!" He got season to let him out at the gas-station after explaining that Gutta was in some heat. The real reason Congo got Season to drop him off was that he spotted bit title Lady Flip, money green 03 Monte Carlo SS

Jeff fiorden edition sitting clean on 24 inch chrome and green rims. Eric and EJ the twins from east Atlanta was pushing her car.

"Yo what ya'll little young ass niggas out here doing with that bitch car?" question Congo, damn never creeping up on the two. But the twins was highly on point even in the mist of there conversation about Amy head game over Jessica's they managed somehow to hear a presence approaching. The twins drawled down on Congo as a resort to his movements. "Oh shit what's up big bruh" greeted EJ putting his .38 Magnum op first.

Eric gave Congo some dap before sliding his own .38 special into his back pocket.

"I need a Ride to the track real quick, ya'll got in I'd drove" Congo told them.

Big title Lady Flip newest Club picture was hanging on the rear-view Mirror. Congo shook his head the girl had 36 triple D but they was sitting perfect on her 5 foot 4 frame. She had no sign of a stomach, wide waist, but hips where flare wider and she was bless to have a heast a "40½ inch chucky ass that set up on her back. They got to the track in record time, the Monte Carlo 55 was fast as a mother fucker. It was at least 15 pimps standing off to the side out of the way.

Even 20 or So of the ho's was turning down tricks to witness the drama a head.

"Oh shit that's my big brother Gutta, let me out this bitch!" Eric said all piped up as he jumped out before the car came to a full stop.

Gutta: BBL

When he saw Eric jump out of Lady Flip car that Congo was pushing, Gutta smiled cause he knew for a fact that True love was about to be pumpkin headed.

"Show time pimping" Smirked Gutta, copping!" Yelled True love

"Nah pimping they think you something to play with" Responded Gotta pointing pass the nigga. Just as True love looked over his shoulder, Eric smiled in his face before telling the pimp.

"You know you done fucked up right?"

The first blow damn near knocked True love to his knees. The other twin EJ hit True love with the butt of his pistol next. True love felt to his knees after that second blow and he dropped the pistol in his hand. Congo jumped out the car laughing, walking up to Gutta and gave him some dap. Then he went to see what True love had in his car, after scooping up the 9mm Berretta 92m pistol the pimp dropped.

"See the different between my pimping and your True love is when I came into this world I came with gone on both hips. We'll never have this problem again, "Us two" mean we got a solid understanding. I got no respect for pimps like you, your bitch is your problem. I'm pimp name Gutta, you will respect my laws on this track or you will get your ass handed to you every time. But the overall lesson for this moment is know who you fucking with" Gutta said.

Congo found a AR. 15 sub-machine gun on the back flobr board, two kilo's of coke, up under the passenger seat, five oz's of bud in the console, $6,150 worth of heroin package in the dash compartment with the extra berretta clip. And when he popped the truck it was a brown paper bag full of money. "Finally the jackpot" said Cong giving Gutta the found it signal.

"Twins let that stupid Motherfucker breath, he's all paid up now" The twins got a few good kicks in still talking shit to True love. They gave him a busted lip, a cracked front tooth, bloody and broken nose and two black eyes.

Its been good seeing you again player, and good looking on the loot True love. Hey maybe at your formal I'll say something good about you instead of pissing in your casket." Gutta said seriously, then waved for his own who's in it was time to relocate for a few hours.

CHAPTER 7

Congo: BBL

"It was $85,000 in the brown paper bag bruh, me, you and Season will get twenty bands each and I'll put twenty in our safe and give the twins five stacks. I'll kept both of the guns, Season got all five oz's; but the Coke and Heroine I'm not sure how you want to play that off just yet" Explained Congo the next morning over breakfast.

Coco had swing by the crib with her sister Peaches and bags full of grocery. Within the last week and a half Congo, Season and Gutta been so busy that niether thought about grocery shopping. The crazy part was cherry did all the shopping for them when they gave her the funds to do so.

"I thought it over last night when I was at my new spot. I'm throw it off on lady Flip Right after Uncle Chicken brick them up. That way we'd all see more profit out the deal and the dog food, I'm give that shit to Keisha from the Bluff after I drop these ho's off at the track" grinned Gotta.

"That's Right I heard you around six this morning breaking ho's in bruh, you coming up fast ain't you? Tested Congo

"Shitd I put pullover in the bag, Ice-cream is my little secretary right now, but I caught these ho's J-10, Bunny and Tiny. A Spanish girl, white girl, and black girl, super package deal. Pullover sex game will make a nigga put babies up in that, J-10 do the anal thing, Bunny nasty as hell and Tiny is the deep throat queen hands down."

50

"Sound high profile to me" winked Congo when Coco strolled out the kitchen with a glasses of juice.

"Don't be telling my man about your out ravenous business, Gutta Ew!" Joked Coco, taking up all the dirty dish's next.

Season: BBL

He had left the crib early to meet New York Black at Zakyby's way out there in love joy. As soon as he seen peaches pull up with her sister in tow season met them at the door, Nobody else was up in the crib beside him, Peaches first mistake was dropping her car keys on the dinner table. The Chrysler 300c drove smoothly plus it had some get up and go to it. He was planning on surprising his main girl about the trip to Myrtle Bench, but she had surprised him six minutes ago through a text.

It read-

"Baby I got to go to seat tale with my family to visit my sick uncle on my mother side, we'd be leaving in the morning."

"Well when I'm done handling my business across town I'm swing by to take you shopping can't have you running around state to state looking like you man less."

"Don't be trying to buy me boy!"

"You already bought"

"Very funny"

"Just be ready when I get there"

"Anything you say baby, xoxoxo"

Season and her signed off just as he was pulling up next to New York Black, black beat up looking late go" model niggan Maxi am. He spotted cherry sitting inside he food joint eating a meal solo. Cherry had called his ass last night after talk with New York Black and gave Season the whole 4.1.1. He jumped out of the 300c and climbed into the Maxi am.

"Yo kid, what's good?" greeted New York Black

"Fast money and slow living is the only way one stay under the radar" stated Season

"I like the way that shit sand yo, so sun you think you can move 100 pounds in a week?"

"It all depends on what you asking for each pound"

"350 pound"

"Sure, I can get rid of 100 pounds within 3 days tops at them prices"

"Get it out the truck on your way out son, and call me as soon as you get my starch"

Season was going to slap only $150 to the ticket and let them go as that. Streets was about to love him especially all the country sides.

Gutta: BBL

After he dropped $47,500 on the Escalade ext for Cherry to push around, Gutta cop a 3 bedroom nice apartment to start stabling his ho's. Gutta left his hos at the track afterward then he called Decator Head ASAP. He had spotted what he was finally looking for and an old black man was behind the wheel of it. Gutta dropped $5,200 to cop the old school Cadillac 2dr vert mother fucker, the snow while paint job with the glitter red scattered Cadillac logos was going to cost $2,500 and $1,100 for the red ragtop alone with the white cross C's by channel.

"Are head, I need my shit hooked the fuck up so cut me some major deals if you want my business right now" Gutta told the well know car thief.

"I got you a soaped up Escalade ext. engine for $1200, four LCD's for $200, A LCD rearview mirror for another 200, back up camera $150, $50 for remote starter $800 for the chrome 24 inches face rims, for all your music set up $1100 and $50 kill switch"

"The shit sound tight but I want one of them X-pods flip out head unit Joints"

"$300 will get you before tomorrow night believe that" boosted Decatur Head.

"Once you done with my whip just drop it off at Mac Neil paint and detail shop"

The best thing about shopping with Decatur he was that the nigga would hook up everything he sold you for free. In the streets of Hustlers that was super player and great business Gutta already had all the rose gold and diamond belza jewels he was going to be rocking in Myrtle Beach. And all his hos was really doing numbers on the track to get the money up for the trip they really wanted to take as well. He spotted a snow bunny with blonds long str-8 hair down her back. She had a body like baye watch Pamala Anderson.

"I'd get back at you my nigga, got money on my mind"

"Do you pimping, I'm out" Decatur head said check in out the white girl as well.

She had strolled into Long horns so he had to make haste across the street so he wouldn't los sight of his prize. He got inside and noticed it wasn't nothing but white folks up in there. That was another thing to about Decatur He'd, the nigga always wanted people he dealt with way out in the country.

"I'm here about the job opening that was posted last week" said the Snow bunny.

"Sorry dear that position was filled a few days ago" The Fat ass guy said liking his lips.

"Without a car I'm always late it seem" Pouted the Snow bunny mostly to herself.

"Have you tried that track stopping place up the road dear?" Questioned the fat goy.

"Right before they sent me down this way" she responded before walking towards the exit.

Gutta waited to she got at the door, the opened it for her. She thanked him and he stepped out behind her.

"I know a job that's paying by the looks if you're interested pretty lady" He threw out there. She stopped dead in her tracks glancing back over her shoulder, staring into his eyes "What kind's job paid people money on their looks, unless you know a modeling business?"

"It's a street modeling business, to better understand it you'll have to come and see it for yourself, and by the way my name is Gutta"

"Hi Gutta, I'm Kimberly" she smiled turning to face him

"So are you interested or not?"

The snow bunny was very interested, so he led her to his temper hot box that Decatur Head set up for him to Ride back to the city in. It was a pink Honda Accord, Clean and fast.

CHAPTER 8

Season: BBL

Three days later and half a day gone by, At 9:48 pm Season was at Vicks house party serving the weed in the break down snacks. He was trying to see every penny out the pound he had Kiwi to break down for him before she left the state. Kiwi big sister kept blowing up his cell phone about her car he took without permission. Key, Key had just cop that Porsche truck mother fucker and he just had to drive it to see what it was talking about. And so far he liked it.

"Say Season let me get five for the $30, home boy" called out young Walt Season gave yang Walt some dap "huh don't come back short next time."

"I got you, I'm just trying to come up off this green snow bunny real quick, home boy"

"Did somebody say snow bunny's!" loud talking as C-2 da mother fucking note joked around doing a little bunny hop dance if you wanted to call it that.

Both young walt and C-2 da mother fucking Note was on the same payee when it came down to white girls. Young Walt hated all white boys that thought they were either hard or black with a passion. But C-2 da mother fucking Note was universal when it came down to dealing with white boys because of what he stood for.

"Bunny's!" laughed young Walt.

Season gave both of them some dap, then bent one ASAP he knew without a doubt how a conversation about snow bunny's was going to last. He weaved in and out the Crowd making player deals

55

to keep his business wanted. Dead or alive, they always fucked with the kid all season around.

"Season where yo girl at?" asked Lexus.

Lexus was a cute Spanish with a 43 inch ass on subll' held by double wide hips, but even so she still was a slim chick, long good wavy hair, dark eyes, a scar going down the left side of face caused by a razor fight she was in back in her home city, she dressed on point and always smelled good but a project chick.

"Which one" Season shot back laughing

"Ya Popi now you know your ass dead wrong for that one" giggled Lexus

"I'm just telling the truth, Lexus. I ain't no player I do fuck a lot on my spare time."

Lexus grinned and said something in Spanish, while pulling him on to the dance floor.

"I don't dance so you must about to throw your ass all over me."

She glanced back over her shoulder, Rolled her eyes at him all seductively, then backed into him before grinding in a huge circular, Motion against his manhood. Season thought Lexus ass was going to be hard because the girl ran track and played soft ball at her school. "News flash" that pat mother fucker was soft, not fether soft like his girl kiwi, but he gave her Cotton status. He stood there brick hard holding on to Lexus waist for support or else all that ass would have slammed him to the ground already.

Congo: BBL

Congo slid into the smoke party an hour and a half late. The hot box he was pushing gave a little trouble, the cutlass ran strong and hard but the flip side of it was hard to crank up most of the time.

He came in with a tall bottle of bray goose in hand tipsy, but slick playing drunk as he scooped out the whole sense for a protection target to come up on. Just on G.P! He seen a dozen ho's that he would love to take up through there but the passion of hitting licks burned hotter than the thought of getting his dick wet. That was because he was capable of hitting the sack with some warm wet-wet on call.

Hitting licks was a challenge, getting pussy was not bottom line.

"Hey Congo" called out Tiffany strolling directly up in his face. Tiffany was Stacy Dash's look alike, but a red bone version with added flavor. Hazel light brown eyes, freshly done micro braids, a tongue ring plus a necklace, watch, bracelet and rings.

"Yo Tiff where you been at baby girl?" He slurred, Keep in up the act.

"Don't baby where you been at me, Congo. You got my number and still haven't called me not even once, what's that about, huh?" She replied.

"I lost it, didn't my boy Season tell you I said get at me?" lied Congo

"He didn't, and I see him a dozen time in the last two weeks"

"I'm sorry for the misunderstanding baby, but we're together now, so give me your number and I'll call you so we can go out for breakfast somewhere nice" Smiled Congo pulling out his phone.

"Nigga don't be laying to me again" she told him before reciting her number.

Congo really wanted to hit that so this time around he was going to do right. He already had her number saved in his phone but he had to play it out so he wouldn't set caught up in his lie. And as of now he had turned her mean mug into a smile.

Smoky: BBL

"Who I be? Smoky" Sung out Smoky coming through the front door loud and very flashy. Smoky was a light skin nigga with good hair and cat eyes. In the streets he was making a name for himself, somewhere in between last month the nigga found a plug on the blow and ex-pill tip. The nigga smoke greenish Dodge charger sat up on some of them 24 inch chrome racing rims.

"Smoky my nigga let a small timer hold something!" shouted Frank from across the Room waving his arms up in the air.

"Huh, come over here and hold my car keys!" responded Smoky holding them up. Frank ran through the crowd pushing folks out of his lane, "Yall move out my damn way!" he was telling them.

"Damn do boy, slow down he aint going nowhere" piped shine Snatching the keys out of Smokey's hand before repaying

"I'm that nigga in training, to the nigga in charge, I'd be sure to let your bitch know that you still love her once I come up in the game my nigga!"

Everybody thought that Frank come back was funny except shine, who shot him the middle finger. The hos crowded around Smoky as if he was a hot rapper or something. They left no room for the stuck up bitches to slid into the mix.

Gutta: BBL

Sitting with the gangsta lean in his Cadillac, Smoking a phat blunt of that Arizona rush with Fat Cat sexy self while listening to Too short in take back ground. Fat Cat was Lady cat's sixth child in line out of nine kids. And lady Cat was still grade a fine. She made some young chicks look bad. Everybody called her Angela Basset, but she was jet black with it, with the extra black lips two gold slugs in her mouth one on each side of her front teeth. All four of her daughters looked just like her.

"What I told you the last time about trying to pimp me Gutta" Joked Fat Cat. Gutta laughed out right, as bad as he wanted to put his little cut buddy on the track just to see what kind a money she'd bring in. Deep down inside he knew that it was all hope.

"But you always talking about doing crazy shit like porn" Gutta said as he passed the blunt.

"Porn is a profession Gutta, Huge difference boy"

"Let make a little an armature flick then"

"How much I get if we do it first?"

"The question is how much you looking for fat Cat?"

"Let's see, I want $9 bucks off each copies that sold, if you agree then we have a deal boy."

Gutta got the blunt black, hit it a few good times while thinking about the sweet profit one could make in the porn world.

"You do know that Flicks are only sold for $10 Fat cat?"

"I know that I'm a big buyer remember" She smiled, reminding him of her 481 fuck flick collection he seen in her bed room.

"And you still want $9, huh?"

"That's the contract, so how you gonna to act boy?"

"I guess I can just make at least 100,000 copies to see my profit then."

"Don't start all that pouting either boy" she teased, playful, smacking him upside the head.

"I'm a name the flick, "Shooters", with lil Wayne track playing at the end.

"That sound like a hardcore flick to me."

"xxx Mother fucker, and you know how Daddy Gutta keep that good sloppy wet pussy skeeting off"

"Whatever boy, I just get to excited because you're silly, plus all hat shit you be talking be kind a funny to me."

Season: BBL

Season sat on the sink in the hall bathroom with his pants down to his knees. He had his chrome and black Walter pole .380 semi-automatic pistol in hand up beside his leg. Just in case some crazy shit come his way. Lexus was super hungry for the dick, deep throating it with no hands, while bouncing, clapping and making her ass walk the dog wildly. Kiwi was great but not this damn great when it came down to giving head.

"Oh you know I'm keeping you fine ass now" Grunted Season.

Lexus pop his wood out her mouth loudly, gripped Him in her hand, stared into his eyes for a quick moment, then went back into action. Stroking him slowly while positioning her mouth near the head. And taunted him by blowing and let spit run down it. Season kept his calm coolness, as he watched and waited for ShowTime. She spat out a replied of Spanish out in the open or talking to his manhood, before licking around the head of it and sucking on it hard.

"Aaaahhh shit! Yo ass that fire for real" Season carried on But Lexus didn't respond because she was to focus on her handiwork. The bathroom door busted open and Season up the strip. Jason, Tasha and Lisa all cocaine partners put their hands up in the air.

"Don't shoot home boy, we thought it was empty up here, our bad Season". Placed Jason staring into the barrel of his pistol since he had the lead of the two girls.

"Damn, I thought you locked the door girl" He question Lexus, gun still aiming.

"Fuck that door, don't you see me suck this dick, shit pop!" she snapped

"Hey, Season" greeted Lisa

"Hi Season" added Tasha

"We all cool, now can ya'll please close the door behind ya" Season stated.

They did just that but then he had to take aim again. Lisa stuck her head back inside smiling; she winked at him while locking the door for them. Once she closed it behind herself.

Season settled back into the groove once again. Season noticed Lexus didn't noticed that the bathroom door opened back up, the second time. Right then and there he made a little mental note to be on point when he was with her.

Lexus Freaky ass wasn't thinking about nothing but getting her freak on. Shit life is great being L.O.V.E, thought Season getting his first of many nuts to come off. And watching Lexus fine ass swallow every bit, not missing a beat or drop.

CHAPTER 9

Mapp: BBL

"Damn Shauty who Robbed you?" asked Mapp

Ten – a- key got up off his love sofa, spitting a glob of blood on to his marble floor. "How the hell would I know, and even if I did, do you really think I'd be here waiting on you to up."

Mapp knew his boy made a good point there, Ten-a-Key was as hard as they come these days. He handed his boy his spare gun, a glock .357 semi auto to be exact.

"The clip is full shawty" stated Mapp

Ten-a-key put a bullet in the chamber "I know my dope as soon as I see it two, who were them nigga was they took 180,000 out my stash spot, Fucking hating ass niggas all over this bitch!"

"Chill with the slick shooting at my city shawty, you knew how this game with the slick shooting at my city shawty, you knew how this game worked before you got deep in it" said Mapp defending his spot.

Ten-a-key eyes Mapp thinking it could have been him I one of them masks, he did fit the profile of the smaller one who never said a world.

"And you can get me off your mind, Shawty" Stated Mapp feeling the bad vibe off the muscle. Ten-e-keys shot back into the back Room while saying "Let's go holla at the smith brothers, if the two niggas act even somewhat strange I'm a pop a cap in them niggas ASAP"

"I'll be out in the car, hurry up Shauty" Mapp responded, heading out to his dark you 95 bubble caprice classic sitting up on 26 inch spinners.

Congo: BBL

"Do me a little favor bruh"

"What dat, Congo?"

"I got $10,000 out the bag, pull over here and let me out, take everything to your spot until I call you."

"Ok but what are you up to, huh?"

"It's a car I'm about to cop, four blocks from, my Myrtle Beach Surprise."

When Big T pulled over Congo gave him some dap then jumped out the car heading about his business. He ended up buying the car for $1200 from an old black man who still thought he was young in the game. Congo got Decatur Head on the horn ASAP and sat up a meeting ASAP. It took him a good hour to ride Out to meet the car thief.

"Olds 442, nice you selling it? Asked Decatur Head

"Nah, I'm get it painted a candy apple green with pearl white stripes. While leather guts with green insert Suds with 4-4-2 imprints. So all I need you to do before that happen is to drop me a brand new Corvette super sport engine under the hood. A Kenwood flip out unit, 2 LED's in the head rest, 4-12 inches kickers in the trunk and Chrome 24 inch rims. Just make sure they aint ugly. Oh why you at it put a Suv flip down LCD unit in the back window 6-6x9.5 2-6x9s in the front doors" Explained Congo.

Out the ten stacks Congo used $9,050 just like that he took Mac neil the money for the pant and gut job to gone ahead and have it out the way. From there Congo was about to head to Big T spot but got side tracked when he spotted a fly ass older chick counting a large stack of money in the driver seat on an all-black on black H2 on 26's spinners. In Congo book bitches with dough could get into if there no mindful.

Season: BBL

Season went shopping, mall to mall buying what he wanted. The Myrtle beach trip was in three days from now and he meant to be super fresh. Though out his shipping spice Season also managed to clock in $6,850

Just off slagging sacks of weed. But he also shoved city love, fronting sacks to the ones who was broke at the time.

"You still going to Myrtle Beach Season?" asked Jamekka

"In three days, why what's happening?"

"Because we wasn't to go to" spoke up Jarita

Jameka and Jarita was known as the Donkey Booty twins, because they both where peacon complexion, short in stature pretty facial wise, But they wasn't real sisters. The two was known for smoken pot on a spiritual level.

"I guess I'd let you two ride out with me, cause I'm a need a driver or drivers until we get three" he had told them.

Gutta: BBL

Chocolate thick ghetto chuck big booty nappy headed self was Gutta new overnight project. He had met her over at Duheem pool party and they hit it off big time. The first thing he did was let her ride around with him so she could see how much money a Ho could clock in on a truck within hours. After the second hour Chocolate was game for whatever. And breaking her in was the best part of the hustle...

"Aaaa hhh daddy that's my spot, oh grand that's my spot!" panted Chocolate in sheer pleasure.

Gutta continued to thrust, driven more and more of his swollen man hood into her guts. Chocolate tightly gripped the red silk bed sheets, tossing her head back crying out as her eyes Rolled up into the back of her head. He began to spank her phat sweaty glazed ass when she announced that she was coming for him. Gutta had to keep self-control form busting all up inside her wet hot kitty to early.

"Mmmm daddy.....!" she moaned out fad on face down. He man handle Chocolate 5'10 figure as if she was a tiny woman in size. Three hours of str-8 sexing her up, doing things no nigga 9 times out 10 had never done to her before. Gutta told her how good her sex game was and mention once or twice how much he loved it. After he flipped her over onto her back, Gutta made love to Chocolate until he had to pull out and skeet all over her stomach and tits. The last major part was when he ran them a bubble bath and bathes her like a true queen.

CHAPTER 10

Congo: BBL

Congo picked up his 442 from Mac Neil shop to take it for a quick spin before parking it. It ran like a champ in his book, and Congo raced it twice for $1,000 just to be sure of it. With his two bands to the good he went ahead and slid to the mall after parking up Coco for the day.

"I can't go to Myrtle Beach with you; I got a job interview this week."

explained Coco.

"You wasn't invited no ways" Chuckled Congo, dodging Coco's punch.

"Boy don't make me get ghetto up in this mall, talking about I wasn't invited to your little trip" She pouted.

Congo pulled her close to him, dropping his arm over her shoulders "Baby don't trip, now you know I got something for us in the long room, just focus on your interview, I'd wish you good luck but you a woman whose beyond lucky so knock them dead."

"Thank you baby, so what trip you got in store for us too?" Coco asked.

"I ain't figured it out yet, buts its between the motel 6 and holiday inn"

"Boy, I'm really hurt you if you keep playing with me" Coco stated while pinching his tight solid Abs.

"Ouch, don't hurt your pretty little fingers, baby" He said giving her a long tender kiss in the middle of the mall floor.

66

The $14,750 he had in his pocket went up in smoke. Congo split it right down the middle. He saw all type of ho's joking him and wishing they we're in his girls heels. They left and went out to Apple bee's her choice on her on expense.

Gutta: BBL

He had cop Cherry a Cadillac ext. truck to push especially for the trip. His Fuck flick with Fat Cat was off the chain. Gutta had this trick ass white boy from Rockdale County make over 30,000 copies for the time being. Fat Cat sold 10,000 of them copies asap right in Atlanta. While he was out Gutta went to pick up the dozen different fitted caps Season had got customized all to his own likening. All the hats represented some type of weed floating around. It was a thousand of each hat and Season was selling them at $15 each. Fat Cat also got a hold of them to and ended up selling 200 each pocketing 2,400 of the top.

"I'm about to kick yo crumb snatching ass out my damn car you keep it up" threatened Gutta.

"What, I can't help it because the street fuck with me the long-strong way." Giggled Fat Cat in the passenger seat counting money.

"I have to sell all those flicks in the city now, before niggas start bootlegging and shit crazy ass girl, I got the white boy making another 30,000 as we speak."

"Shit, I wasn't talking about the bootleg hustle."

"I know that's why I'm the thinker of this relationship, now get on your phone and make us some mover sells."

"Okay, daddy" Joked Fat Cat doing as she was told.

CHAPTER 11

They went to Myrtle Beach five cars deep. There beach strip was Jam packed with type of Fly ass cars, trucks SUV's and vans. One couldn't really tell you was flexing or front my because everybody looked like money. It was lot of folks Driven around for hours looking for living spots for x-amount of time they were going to be enjoying the sight. And to over kill the whole game, there whole crew was pent house stunting.

Congo suggested that they throw a party in the pent house. Season know the outcome of throwing a party so soon and said a penthouse party will be there heading out plan. Gutta wanted to work his on the beach strip. Season told him it wouldn't be wise especially since no one knew nothing about the Justice system. The whole crew just ended back on the beach strip either walking or pushing there car's. They got off the fuck flicks, the hats and hot jewelry.

Half ass naked bitchs was popping pussy all up down the strip, Bad girls, College girls and Good girls was all out soul searching for love. Lame ass niggas was fallen into them traps Caking the ho's and ready to take them to meet the mom duke. But that ain't how Season, Gutta and Congo rolled the dress. The trio made freaks domes them up on the spot, accepting numbers from all over the state plus made promises that was already broken.

CHAPTER 12

Congo: BBL

It took everything in his power to fall back last night, with so many fronting niggas flossing on the strip Congo could have been plucking them left and right like Ripe grapes. See it was super easy for Big T to enjoy himself because his patient was sky high. To Big T when it came down to Jacking niggas his big homie felt like every target wasn't a good target. Bull Shit!

Congo was still highly pissed that he ended up letting smoky escape his side of the board game. Smoky had got away by the hair on his chiny-chin-chin. But on the flip side Congo had his little sis Cherry on her second important job. Cherry Chocolate was the team and they worked good together. Them ho's was weave out the poor niggas from the rich niggas.

Fat Cat: BBL

She had Jolo, Bunny and Tiny helping her sell he fuck flicks, they were making a killing to especially on getting the rich niggas to buy the autograph ones.

"Say ma, how much it's gonna cost me to make flicks with you, huh?" asked the nigga behind the wheel of a Bentley coupe.

"100,000 plus high maintained fees," Fat Cat told him seriously.

"Damn ma you think you worth that much for real, huh?"

"You bought the flick check it out; you'll see I'm worth every penny"

It was four nigga's in the Bentley Coupe, the passenger in the front slid he copies into the D.V.D player, As they skip through senses Fat Cat brained worked fast.

"For $20,000 ya'll can Run a train on anyone of my employees, this Tiny, Bunny and that's J-10"

"Bet that we'd take J-10, but I'd drop $20,000 more to do the same with bunny and Tiny."

So they went back to the Bentley Boys Hotel Room which was suite and Fat Cat made money. Pimping was infect a great money make hustle.

Season: BBL

He had got up early along with Pullover crazy ass. They hit the strip selling his hats and to see what was going on for tonight. Everybody seemed to be passing out party flyers. Pullover had ran into a major club owner who was really into her the long way. The club owner was about 45 years old give or take, plus he was married but that didn't stop pull over fast ass from playing up under the man.

"Anybody over told you that you look like Trina?" asked the club owner.

"Yeah, sometimes but that's my big cousin my father and Trina's mother are brothers and sisters" lied pull over but at the end of take day she locked like money so her story was believable.

"So how long you two going to be in my town, pretty lady?"

"Two weeks, but it's actually ten of us, nine girls and G-smooth is the only guy we trust to ride out with us."

"Okay, I see like just incase ya'll get into something yall can't handle"

"That's exactly right, like getting married" piped up season to put the icing on the cake and the old man had the look in his eyes to call home divorce his wife and sweep Pull over off her feet's.

Gutta: BBL

Pimping was in full effect as Gutta took his game to the strip looking for some ho's to take back home. He had Ice-cream at his heel and Tweety putting in foot work. He had told Tweety crazy ass to find sisters-in-laws and the ho's started selling pussy on the strip.

"That's a hard head ho right there I swear" Gutta stated

"But if you think about it daddy, she's charging double for what she'd make at home on the track."

Board day light Tweety had a dozen or so niggas wasting in line to sample her goods. Tweety was killing two birds every time with one stone. She was sucking a nigga up on the car hood whale a nigga was hitting her from the back. And he had to stay close to his crazy ass ho so the police wouldn't bust her for prostitution. The crazy part was Tweety had created a large crowd and in this crowd was other nasty batches trying to cut in.

Them the bitches Gutta set his pimping to ASAP and four of them ate up his game. Moo-Moo who was built like Buffy the body but had a cutter face. Jade who was built like Blake China before she got pregnant with Rob's baby and had a smaller head.

Fat girl was just a name because she wasn't fat at all, she could go for Ariel Meredith twin.

Pebbles looked like Hillary Fisher the curve model but she was black. So within three hours everything played out for the good in Gutta's book.

CHAPTER 13

That even the whole crew met back up to hang out as a group. They found a spot to set up for a few hours, Gutta, Gig T and Congo was running the free for all liquor bar out there trunks. Everyone had their own hidden agenda but worked the Sense as a happy go lucky green around the car kid. A nigga got so pissed he went around getting in folks faces, threatening them because someone stole his drop top chevalier ss.

Then another nigga wigged out about his Belair being stolen hours later and started shooting at crowd of niggas who his crew had words with earlier. During the panic Big T and Congo with masks on dunked a Miami nigga with dreads and a mouthful of gold slugs into the trunk of his own Dunk. The Miami nigga was riding solo with $150,000 worth of bling-bling on like fuck the world I'm untouchable.

Cherry had got Congo car and Chocolate took Big T's. Gutta was the one who lead the way to pullover's new club owner sugar daddy club. She got them all into V.I.P and they were treated like the rich + famous. And two hours later pull over got into a first fight with a big booty Redbone who was all up on her sugar daddy. The red bone was losing grooved but Gutta slid in to save her face.

CHAPTER 14

Congo: BBL

He sat on the hood of the Donk counting out the money from the Miami nigga's pockets and personal shaving kit boy. Congo couldn't stop laughing and his crazy ass crime partner Big T had heat for niggas from Miami ever since the Atlanta us Miami war back in the days.

"Stall him out Debo" Joked Congo

"What? Shawty fuck this buster, always think there better than us, they gonna respect this real city shit or get fucked up every time, you hear me in there chump its city Debo!" Big T beated on the trunk of the Donk.

"Jit I aint got no beef with niggas form Atlanta, I swear on my kids!" Shouted the Miami nigga from the trunk.

"Stop lying chump we beef in everything basketball, football, baseball, track + field and believe me I know you ain't never went for none of my home teams."

"I like the Braves, Jit"

"Name five players"

"Umm..."

"Umm, I know that's right lying mother fucker!"

Congo slid off the hood of the Donk saying Gone head and let the nigga out, we good" Big T opened the trunk and pulled the nigga out of it by his shirt and dreads. Congo gave the Miami nigga $100 to catch a Gray hound back home ASAP. They were parked across the street from it and it took for and half hours before the bus to Miami took off. Congo and Big T was planning on selling the Donk to a rich nigga in the city. Knowing they could at least get $30,000 out of Shawty's Donk.

The Don was just that clean hands down it could be on a show room floor. Candy paint, wood grain steering wheel, plush leather seats, 454 crate chrome engine up under the hood, eight T.V's, beat in the trunk and 26 inch Rims to match the paint job.

CHAPTER 15

Gutta: BBL

"On the real shawty you to be running around fighting in clubs and shit" Gutta told her after taking her out to his Cadillac. She sat in the passenger seat with her arms folded across her tits. "And what do you care I'm not your girl or anything?"

"Chill on that hard shit shawty it's Spring Bling which mean a time to party, and enjoy all the wildest pleasures we could imagine."

"What's is your name boy?" She questioned

"Gutta" He smiled, checking ole girl out.

She looked like me rapper the brat but with a 48 inch fat ass no lie. Her name was Razzle and she was born and raised in Myrtle Beach. That was the cake but the icing was when Gutta got to beat that wet, wet up in the front seat.

Season: BBL

He Was balling out of control but that's what he was there for. Plus on top of that Season saw how Gutta's ho's was working the floor, pick pocketing nigga's, or letting niggas get wasted before they just out right go into their pockets. Within the first hour Gutta ho's had bought Season over $28,000 to hold.

"So you from Atlanta huh?" Asked a nigga shorter than him

"From the heart of it, why what's up shawty?"

"I'm from Boston, me and my brother's be trying to buy some weight, what's yall prices hitting on out there?"

"It depends on what you trying to cop and who you getting it form"

"Oh, I get what you saying-so if I swing through can me and my brothers use your face, the sweeter the deals the move money you'd make as a middle man."

Season thought that little bit over and decided to run with self Depe boy. Afterward Season let these two super thick and cute chicks approach him since they were on their grown woman shit. And at the end they went for his slick words so he could get double head in V.I.P.

CHAPTER 16

For two weeks strong all they did was party like Rock stars, Came up on some good licks, Fucked with some bad batches, met some Hustlers for some future business arrangements. Gutta on the other hand lost all his new ho's except pebbles so he did come up until his Cadillac got stolen. And he shot two niggas out of anger. Big T had left three days before everyone else because he had to drive the Donk back to the City.

Congo stayed looking for any last minute lick but did find a good one. That was easy or that made him want to go all out. But overall it was good to be safe at home one again.

CHAPTER 17

Season, Congo and Gutta sat in the living room with the lights off in the whole apartment. The Floor model flat screen 60 inch TV. was the only thing on at that very moment. They was lounging around each smoking a blunt to the head. Gutta had a bottle of red wine between his legs. Congo was slipping away a bottle of Volka and Season had his can of red bull.

"We either go hard or get the fuck out the streets, homies" State Gotta

"Me and Big T got some more shit coming up soon, bruh" Congo told them.

"That's what's up, I'm get some ho's on the track, plus I think my new Ho pebbles going to do stupid good numbers" Cheesed Gutta to the point that you could see his whole rose gold grille.

"I heard down in millegavile ga, white girls got ghetto asses and, Bunny brings in $2,000 aday easy so you can just imagine what one with a phat ass will make."

"Yeah I know Right that Just mean more money and more pimping going on, on my end."

Hot: BBL

Mean while Boo Boo and Hot had got into it again. Boo Boo had done got on Hot ass, as if he was a ragdoll. She didn't let up until her baby sister strolled through the front door. Phat back and two of her girl friends was stopping by to pick up Boo Boo's son for the weekend.

"Boo Boo stop don't you see he had enough!" Screamed phat back as she got between the two.

"Nah, move cause I done told his punk ass never hit me again" cried Boo Boo trying to stop around her sister and kick her baby daddy in the head.

Phatback could careless to what happen to hot ass but she didn't want to be riding way out to the back woods country side, to be visiting her in prison if she messed around and killed the nigga. As she glanced down at hot who was in the fatal position all bloody. Then she looked up at her big sister bloody face and got pissed but held her emotions in check.

"Slim, Prada ya'll take my sister out to my car, I'm go grab my nephew real quick."

When Phatback came strolling out the bedroom with was now laying on his back eyes wide open.

"Nigga sooner or later somebody gang do something evil to you, Hot"

"Fuck you ugly bitch"

"I might be ugly but I'm a Boss bitch, believe that with yo broke as, even though I hate you Hot I still wish you'd get your shit together for lil Hot sake. And I left $650 on the bathroom counter go out and buy you a pack, start off small and work your way to the top for once, everybody can't be a stick up kid in the game."

CHAPTER 18

Congo: BBL

A month went by fast and somewhat shit got out of hand on Season end. Some dope boy name DJ and some of his little nigga had jumped on Gutta.

"Congo when are you going to leave the streets alone, huh?"

"Coco you know this is how we eat and my hustle is how you get all of that fly ass gear you been rockin lately".

"Baby I know that but I just don't want to lose you"

"Coco I ain't going nowhere just stop warring so much"

"Aye, Big T out front and he said you need to come on ASAP!" said season walking past the bedroom.

Congo Jumped out the bed with Coco and Ran outside, Big T yelled out the car window and told Congo to get dressed. Congo didn't waste no time he ran back to the room and changed into all black and grabbed his Desert Eagle. He kissed Coco on the forehead and told her that he would be right back. He wasted no time getting back to the with Big T.

"What's going on bruh?" Congo asked.

"Man I just saw a move that might sat us str-8 for a minute."

"Okay that's what's up but where is it at?"

"It's just two exits down from here."

Big T told Congo all about the licks as they drove the high way. As they arrived at their location they scan the area to check there ins and outs. Big T parked the car and they jumped out, Congo and Big T scale the wall of the builder. As they got to the back of the ware house they seen a big drug deal going down. It was one of the biggest that they had ever seen.

"Aye bruh that's a lot of people back here and I only brought my desert Eagle"

"Man bruh to be honest when I drove by it was only two cars back here, I didn't know all these Folks was coming"

"Man bruh we might have to sit this one out and just pick a car and follow it"

"Yeah, you right Congo cause this shit would end real bad for us"

"Aye what the hell are ya'll doing back here?" Yelled sure white man in a suit.

Big T turned around and fired his gun hitting the man in the chest, as he hit the ground Big T and Congo run over to take his mi 16 off his shoulder. Congo grabbed the mi 16 from Big T then ran back to the edge of the building. everybody was in the same spot as they were like nothing happen.

"Look Big T we done came to far now so we got to make it happen"

"I know bruh, the white dude ducked everything up just then"

"Ok well look on the count of 3 we gone run off, once behind the building we gonna shout out freeze police, and that should make everybody run or shoot so either way get Ready".

"If they run what we do?

"Hell we go after the one we think got the most money"

"Ok bet"

"1..... 2.... 3.... Police don't move!"

"Freeze DEA!" yelled out Big T

Congo and Big T came from around the building and everybody disburse in different directions. Congo slipped and squeezed the trigger and it started a miniature war. Congo and Big T hid beheaded a green dumpster bullets was flying everywhere. Every now and then Big T and Congo would send a few shots out.

Congo only heard two cars drive out the parking area, so it had him confused if everyone else was shot or just aint made it to their vehicle yet.

Pebble: BBL

Pebbles sucked the tricks man hood with a burning passion, while the guy reclined in his seat, Moaning anal grunting. All he loud slurping sound effects she made, plus the fact pebbles had the blacked biggest soup coolers on the track. Kept tricks coming both ways. If you feel what I mean?

"That feel so...good lv, shit eat this ....dick...up!" cried the trick.

Her head was going for $150 on the track, just shy of $50 short of that wo Deep throat Monique. The trick figured pebbles woman hood which coasted him $20, legs spread open for the trick as she simultaneously rocked the tip of his manhood and jerked him the long way. It only took her 15 minutes to get the trick nut, tossed the spent condom out the window smiling.

Damn shawty you got some pretty ass lips for real" the trick told her trying to catch his breath.

"So when I'm see you again big boy" She question seductively pulling down her leather skirt.

"Probably tomorrow at the same time, just gotta go make this quick play here and there to keep up this madness you putting me through, trying to set at you on the seal" expressed the trick.

The old head been trying to get at her for the last month and a half now, a trick ass nigga who confused his love to every ho he paid for pleasure.

"I know how you feel but I'm happy with the life I'm living right now, but I enjoy your company more then I love to admit too, Tommy."

"And I love spending time with you to pebbles, you be careful out here okay?" Tommy said as he started the ignition.

"Okay, see you tomorrow Tommy."

When the pearl green Mercedes Benz E-class pulled away from the curb, Pebbles strolled back the two blocks to the track. But on the next block over she spotted her daddy's Cadillac parked off to the side. Hazard lights flashing, code for hot track ahead. Pebbles made haste to the car and climbed into the back seat and was greeted by three of her sister-in-laws.

J-10, Bunny and Tiny was all counting out how much profit they each made the four hours they been on the Ho stroll. And pebbles followed the Normal Routine suit, as her daddy filled her in on what was happening. "White girl, big booty Judie and the new Mexican chick Angel Rose got locked up." Once all his Ho's was off the track Gutta felt a little more at case.

Apple bottom and Baby phat both paid him $200 each for a much needed ride as for away from the track as Possible. Bird was their pimp a older nigga who been in the game at least for ten years top. Gutta hauled his whole business off to a different location to clock that pleasure money.

Cherry: BBL

Cherry and Chocolate was the main attraction at the private Bachelor party. They was paid at the door the promise $1,500 just for showing up. Other then themselves it was a dozen clean str-8 lace strippers there getting money. And them bitches was up in there really hating hard. What made Cherry and chocolate stranded out was simple business since their daddy taught them.

The both of them held no punches when it came to treating trick ass niggas, specially on a girlfriend, boy friend level sort to speak. And giving a trick whatever they wanted, As long as they paid the price to be the shot caller. That was one of Gutta's M/O's.

Detroit Blue had threw the party in his $750,000 loft in Buck head. In the wide open spacious living Room. Cherry really bought out the big bucks, when she pulled out the red dildo and sexed Chocolate with it, Plus ate her sister-in-law the fuck out.

Pussy she enjoyed with a intense since of Hunger. There was twenty hustlers in attendance and they kept tripping the two on the thick plush bear Rug generously. Nothing but booty shaking Music blared out of the speakers, and all the strippers still in their G-Strings made the best of it. Well most of them...

The top notch baldest looking bitch there was Remy hands down. Gorgeous and guilt just like Ki-toy that video model. Her hair, nails and G-string was top of the line shit. She was Bentley Blue, who was the one getting married in three days side candy. So she was really pissed the fuck off when he yelled out just as the music went off.

"These two bitches on this floor going to be the death of my pockets!" he stated as he threw another stack of hundred dollar bills.

"That redbone know she's a monster too!" Yelled out another nigga throwing up $20's

"That Rose gold grille put the icing on the cake!" add another one

"Who called my name?" teased the light bright almost white Mc-Trina pull over that ass to fat look alike.

"I called you if that's really your name" Stated cheesy unbarring her face from between Chocolate's thick thighs, looking at the stripper while licking her lips.

"Don't be scared now cake!" a nigga blurted out.

"Yeah, Shawty get into action so I can break you off some of this paper with your fine ass" Shawty Blue waved the six large stacks of bills in his hands at her.

"I really don't get down like that fells" she explained, as her eyes took towards the girl on her back moaning out that she was coming as the other girl kept dong her with a big dildo.

"Now that's how good olc pussy get wet, see I can wake up to that" Shawty Blue stated.

"You ain't never lied" giggled cherry, then said "Cake don't make me have to come over there and get your fine ass."

The girl was teasing her while making eye contact. Cake couldn't stop blushing, she didn't know what to do at this point she needed the money from this party to pay all her late ass bills. Detrot Blue threw a spare of the moment party every other month. The money always came in handy, And if she turned around to flee now cake wonder if she ever be invited to another one of his parties. What use to be str-8 clean lace for us was just changed by the two new hicks. The game was now hard core xxx Rated.

"Shawty, let me see what you working with." Shawty Blue gave her a little push forward and when she glanced back at him he winked. When Cake got in the mist of the new girls on the floor they pulled her dawn to join them. Remy wanted to throw up all over the floor. When both new girls began taking turns eating cake out. "Nasty ass ho's trying to pull all of us up under that fucking rainbow wave" She was Ragging in her head.

"Shit Cake you going home with me Shawty once all this shit over with!" Shawty Blue shouted out excitedly making it Rain heavily.

Congo: BBL

It was Congo lucky night for real him and Big T had counted to sixty before peeping around the cohere. Dead mother fuckers was scaled out all over the warehouse. Some of them was Right at their car door but still didn't make it. Big-T took off in a dead run make sure that nobody was playing dead. Two niggas he had to put a single bullet in there Domes.

Mean while Congo was checking trap coming up on a duffle bag full of money and three duffle bags full of cocaine kilo's. He gave Big T the signal to let him know that the loot was secured. Big T nodded smiling, he had all the guns men assault rifles and sub-machine guns cradle in his big arms. They left up out of there wide open not looking back once.

"I'm going stupid shopping for the fame" stated Congo smiling ear to ear.

"I'm cop my girl that house she want so she can stop talking about, I don't never buy her what she really want" Explained Big T.

"What about all them fur coats you be buying her?"

"That's what I asked her and she said that it's my job to make her look like a million dollars since I want to stay in the streets."

"Oh, now that's really cold" laughed Congo

"You know Coco be all up in her sister head about us trying to get both of us out the streets for good, but I don't know what we'd be even good at if we decided to go legit."

"Shidd whatever it is as long as it got something to do with guns then I'm cool with it" expressed Congo.

Gutta: BBL

"Fuck you Gutta! Why you trying to play us like we're stupid or something" shouted Apple bottom from the front seat

"Fuck all that shit you ho's talking, this my track I made this one come back alive for my ho's to clock. My dough ya'll to wo's want to test out my shit its going to cost both of you $1,500 each, bottom line."

"Now you know if we give you any more of our daddy's money, he'd whoop our asses damn near to death" Whined Baby phat.

"look this my money out here, that's the point I'm trying to make, so I'd be sharing when I don't have to".

Apple bottom smacked her teeth, rolling her eyes at Gutta before addressing her sister-in-law "What you want to do girl?"

"I don't really see no choice in the matter, if we want to make that money" responded Babyphat Rolling her neck and eyeing Gutta.

"Yall two Ho's really be fronting too much."

"Fronting about what huh?" Question Apple bottom folding her arms

"Yeah, really want this pimp juice over here, I see yall stable slick falling off lately, my Ho's nails and hair stay did up to show case, and if it ain't channel, Gucci or prada my Ho's aint wearing it. Cherry my bottom bitch and she rolling around in a Cadillac Escalade eat on 26 inches spinners. I'd cop you two a Escalade to push, so while ya'll out.

there making that money think about ya'll future lifestyle"

Apple bottom got out then let Baby phat out the seat. They walked shoulder to shoulder talking until they made it down to the track. Gutta smiled already counting the two new ho's in his stable. He didn't flip run always because of their ages most of the time, but really it was because they didn't have nowhere to live, Cherry was the only one really who was allowed to stay with him.

The 3 bedroom apartment that he had cop had filled up quick. He knew he'd either was going to have to buy another one or get a duplex. Cocotte shared a room with Cherry a lot lately. J-10 and Bunny had a room together and pebbles shared a room with Tweety from time to time. Big Booty Jodie and Angel Rose both still stayed at their peoples crib.

Gutta will just have to cop another one of them apartments in the same complex for the time being. He was going to send Cherry out to find a big enough spot for all his Ho's. But as of now he had to get in contact with his usual lawyer, to see what was the deal with his two new Ho's.

CHAPTER 19

Hot: BBL

He been eating real good, 17 oz's of dope to be exact. Plus he was pushing a brand new Dodge Magnum sitting on 24 inch chrome rims. His new girl Jessica had two small kids and Hot kept them fresh to death. And the crazy part was, out of all the money he was seeing he still haven't spent a single penny on his baby moma or his own son.

"Man you tripping, I seen Boo Boo hop out of that pussy ass nigga whip to cop a room last night" said Q

"What pussy ass nigga, It's so many hell I done lose count?" Smiled Hot as he leaned back into his seat.

"Man shawty, you know that nigga Congo your trying to see"

Hot raised up in his seat damn near knocking the fire off the blunt into his lap. Instead it flew onto the floor. He knew Boo Boo ass was out trembling around the floor. He knew Boo Boo ass was out trembling around but not with that nigga Congo.

"Shawty kill the fire before it go a blazing in this mother fucker!"

"Oh shit!" Jumped hot after nothing his floor matt was on fire. Hot was about to down bad that nigga Congo once and for all for fucking up his life.

Chip: BBL

Chip pushed up on his plog on the fuck shit early that morning. New York Black had just dropped Cherry off at the mall too, so she could spurge on a $100,000 shopping spree.

"Man, big bruh that's the ho that be fucking around with Season, you know that right?"

"Yo son are you sure of that?"

"Positive! What she told you about him, that they were kin or something, shit if you went for that shawty then take my old lady number down. Shit I want in too." Joked Chip

Chip was trying to knock Season ass out the box so he'd be the man with the loud, plus he could go back up on his tickets. Season was in the way and it was only one way to get rid of his smooth slick ass.

Season: BBL

Up early in the morning Season got himself together smoked a blunt to the head while rubbing his girl kiwi, phat soft ass as if it was a magical globe. She was laid up on her stomach sound asleep, they didn't get into anything last night. Kiwi job at the strip clob and her college classes was the number one and two time consuming in her life right now. Which was fine with Season because he played the streets like Letron James basket ball. That's right he was all over that mother fucker wide open. Beep.. Beep..Beep, a text came through to his cell phone. He slid off the bed to retrieve it off the tall dresser.

"Shawty, I need four oz's of some decent weed to somke, but I need 50 ex-pills with that, this your little bruh Young Music fuck with me!" It had read

"That's a bet give me ten minutes and meet me at our usual spot" He texted back, then put the phone on his hip.

Season strolled out the bedroom locking Kiwi bedroom door behind himself. Down the hall in the master bedroom was Teasie, Kiwi's older roommate and stripper partner, getting her guts beat, inside out by her sugar daddy. He grinned and snatched up the Lexus sc 430 keys off the dinner table. Text "driver should have been my middle name" He sanded as he headed out the two bedroom town apartment.

Gutta: BBL

The only reason Gutta was still up was because his Ho's wanted to stay on the stroll around two in the morning. It got really live with tricks coming and going freely. Older white guys pulling up in Jag's, Lexus, BMW's and Benz's. Two old white guys in the back in the back of limo's. A Black nigga from cali pushing a blue lambo. And a fat ass nasty sloppy Mexican pushing a 05 Cadillac. Clk Groups.

Gutta wanted sthat Cadillac so he put Tweety on the Job. The car was silver but he wanted it a pearl red, but keep the guts silver, throw some 22's on it.

"Hello?" Gutta answered hoping it was someone who had info on Bird where about.

"You up, too, huh?" Chuckled Season

"Pimping is a all job, you aint heard"

"Not in my field, so I probably looked over that message, but look I need 50 pills to handle a play quick."

"They all on me, you can come to the track or I can meet you somewhere."

And of course Season who had all the sense got Gutta to meet him at the drop off spot too. But before Gutta peeled he got all the money his ho's had on them just in case any fouls play what on before he came back.

Brid: BBL

Bird kept out the loop for a week and a half.

Ignoring phone calls and trying to just forget about the ho stroll all together. His new business with Gutta was beyond out of hand as of now. Bird and his five young goons had actually Jumped on Gutta at the track about taking Apple bottom and Babyphat.

They young crazy wild nigga and his two home boys came at Bird baring Ak-47, Knocking off there of the old pimps young goons off in the mist of the shootout. Bird had twenty-two missed calls, nine of them was threatening messages form Gutta, he young nigga wanted some str-8n. Something in Bird made her extremely nervous as he travelled in the limo on his way back to city that he loved in many ways. He was quiet, notching his bottom peering out the corner of her eye at him.

"Bitch you got something on your mind you want to say, then say it!" shouted Bird.

Mercy who was never the one to back down, turned to face him in her seat." I told you that them little pretty ass niggas soft, you didn't want to listen to me, whole you been down in Millersville go. Somebody broke into our house and took everything we had to our name and not only did we loss Apple bottom and Baby Phat, count Candy, Beaches, Rhonda and Tracy out too, other pimps talking a scared pimp is nothing more then a bitch himself, I got there other 15 Ho's in line but that's only by a thread, Hustlers putting out on the streets that you smoking crack now, and I really don't know what to do cause of lately I don't know if you are coming or going daddy."

"It's going to be all good baby, daddy going to shoot the one with the young punk, and show three niggas out here that shit aint sweet" Bird expressed nervously

Gutta was the only young head on the track who holded weight with a real stable. Other young niggas came and went bringing G-freaks or Runways through to make a quick come up. The pimps hated when the young niggas came onto the track because of the drama they brought alone with them. But the pimps also loved to see the young niggas too. Because all the tender meat they supplied the stroll with.

The real pimps ended up with the young niggas left over's every time. And Bird remember way back when Gutta was one of the dumb ass young nigga, just in it for the quick come up. Shit had really changed in the last two years.

CHAPTER 20

New York Black: BBL

The middle-aged bad headed Jet black NYC nigga whose been supplying plenty pounds of that BC Dro throughout the city of Atlanta for months, now, still couldn't resist cherry's sex appeal. He was always go dazzled by her long dreads with her red tips, red complexion glossy pink lips and 8 open face Rose gold grille that he fell victim to lust every time.

She was a tid bit thicker then petile and clad in some which dasiy dukes, her red baby doll T-shirt barly could restrain her ripe melon tits. The girl was long legged stood back on her knees, slick the bow legged type. So the 4½ inch heels looked tasteful on her overall appearance. Her fire red complexion with tattoos and glossy dark pink lips with that designer grille cursed his dick to get a stupid erection.

He had met his Arinazo Mexican plug at club Magic city, to pick up the 100 pounds of Airazona Rush whish was a loud type of mid that had a mean kick to it. New York Black spotted the red bone at the grey hand station, carrying a single duffle bag. After pulling up on her he found out that she was from Miami fla and Came up to see what Hot Atlanta was talking about.

He already had a wife at the crib so all he really wanted to do was get a quick blow job and smash.

them guts before leaving her ass at a motel somewhere.

"Yo you smoke Shorty?

"I don't smoke no bull shit nigga" Strawberry responded

"All I smoke is the best, this right here I just got its called Airazona Rush, Shorty some real Mexican but" bragged New York Black Smacking her teeth al sexy like, strawberry smiled "And you better not have a little dick either."

New York Black almost choked off the thick smoke in the worse way, eyes watery and red because of Shorty bold bluntness. strawberry put him in the mind of that porn queen Pinky, or older thicker Cherry with her shit talking ass cause she knew her pussy was fire. Being distracted smoking weed and talking nasty with her shit talking ass cause she knew her pussy was fire. Being distracted smoking weed and talking nasty with Strawberry. New York Black didn't even notice the all black Chrysler 300 following him.

He parked his black on black G-wagon that was sitting on sprell wells in a vacant park parking lot 15 minutes later. It was two box Cheuys, a bubble impala and regal scatted parked, out there too. But they were all empty and been striped by car thieves.

"Don't act shy now nigga, pull that dick out so I can see how big my challenge is" teased strawberry

New York Black high ass quickly un buckled his Lovie Vutlon pants, pushing them down to his knees alone with his boxer briefs. His hard six inch manhood became exposed an strawberry went to work ASAP. By gripping it and squeezing him just enough to make him lift up in his own seat.

"Don't let me find out that you a up North soft nigga" laughed strawberry, spotting the two dark shadows approaching the driver side window.

"Aint nothing soft about New York Shorty, we created the word hard you didn't know"

The driver window shattered in wards loudly, steel smashing into glass, Ruining the show case Jeep image.

"What the fu"

"Bitch ass nigga, shut the fuck up and get out here!" Roared Big T Snatching New York Black ass from the driver seat violently and throwing the nigga to the pavement.

Dazed, New York Black was scared and bucked as he stared up at the two gun man. They had him sitting on his bare ass with too loaded Glock 40's at his head.

"Shawty, you must think shit a game in the city, coming and going as you please, cutting niggas off like your bitch ass really got that choice, News flash up North ass nigga, down here we call our city Hot Atlanta" stated Congo, then unloaded the whole clip into New York Black.

"This was called a statement murder."

Before the shooting had started strawberry had climbed into the back and found all the dope. Big T crazy ass snatched the bloody lovie vutlon pants off the dead nigga, laughing getting the money out the pockets before tossing the pants on top of the New York nigga head. Congo got all the Jewellery off New York Black's person. After they laded all the dope into the 300c they peeled with Strawberry behind the wheel.

Season: BBL

"Look, we're not about to have this conversation about my car, aint nobody tell you to go and were yo shit."

Season wasn't trying to hear all that from his girl. Who was extremely beautiful, light skinned, green slanted eyes, Chinese-Jamaican 5'4 with a 45 inch bubble butt. Stripper/ college girl that was trying to run game about his shit. Kiwi was the perfect model to have in a str-8 stunting Magazine, nothing was fat on her but that ass and cat print.

"You get on my damn nerves sometimes I swear it" Whine Kiwi

"Good, its time to pay you back for all the shot nerves I got from fucking with you for this long" Season shot back all cool.

"So how am I suppose to get back and forth from school and work, baby?"

"Stop all that whining kiwi, for I trade yo ass in for a Japanese white girl."

Kiwi opned he mouth, couldn't find a word to express her feelings, so she closed it and just narrowed her eyes at her four year off and on boyfriend.

"Maybe her name will be something exclusive like Dragon Lilly."

He said out loud, busting open a Swiss roll little Debbie cake and spooning peanut butter them with his high ass. Season at two more of them cakes the same way before going off to answer his metro Pcs. He had got rid of every pre-paid phone because of the foot bills.

Being the weed man mint it was a lot of people who was in demand of some green, to blaze up. And season supplied over 100 mother fucker in the city, that's not including their friends. This white boy in Rock dale county wanted to cop ten pounds of Kush. Season was going to charge the crack $650 for each pound. But it was going to be ten pounds of that Gangster-mid instead because that's all he had on hand at that very moment.

His Kush and Chocolate plug dumb ass got caught up in a raid a week ago, so Season been out of luck on finding another suppler as of now. But he didn't sweat the issue, because his home boys. Kept his operation flowing in some type of form or fashion. Season headed up stairs with Kiwi on his heels he needed to prepare for the road trip.

As he got to the second flight of steps, it was clearly what his home boy Gutta had going on.

"That boy need to stop turning all these girls out" giggled Kiwi

Loud moans and grunts was booming form behind his Roommate bedroom door as they passed by it. Inside his own bedroom season glanced back at his girl, eyes zooming in on her very noticeable hard nipples.

"Go sit your hot ass down somewhere" He tested her

"What are you talking about ba-by!" Purred out Kiwi

Gutta: BBL

Inside the bedroom, Gutta was all up in Ice-cream young tight, sticky, wet, hot guts making streets love to her. Ice-cream pulled him deeper into her, screaming out that she was about to come for him. The head board slammed up against the wall as she squeezed her legs lightly around his waist.

"This daddy Gutta's pussy, huh?" grunted Gutta

Ice-cream nodded her head eyes closed, squealing out in pleasure as he pounded into her with quick short strokes. Beneath him, Ice-cream moaned and panted, her orange hair spilled around her beautiful face and pillow. There sex was loud in the air of the room. Gutta netted right behind her, then forced himself to pull out of her, sighing as he rolled onto his side and pulled her into his arms.

"We gotta go check up on the girls, daddy" breathed out Ice-cream.

"In a minute baby, In a minute" smiled Gutta.

Kissing the back of her bare shoulder passionately. He was gonna have to trick Ice-cream on the track real soon, she had that cat that will make a trick want to keep on scratching.

Congo: BBL

Congo used his key to let them into the apartment. They set, the loot, they got off of New York Black on top of the glass top dinner table. Strawberry was put to the task of counting the money while Congo and Big T seen to how many pounds they came up on. "There's $15,046 here" stated Strawberry fanning herself with the stack of money griming.

"Split that two ways for me, big sis" Congo told her and she did just that.

At the end Big T drove away with $7,523 and 25 pounds to his name. When the coast was clear Strawberry pulled out the 9 oz's of coke, $21,500 and chrome .357 magnum she found up under New York Blacks driver seat when she searched the jeep.

"Now we just gotta get rid of all this dead niggas Jewelry big sis." Smiled Congo holding up the heavy platinum diamond neckless.

"We can hold on to it until we take that trip to Mississippi!" winked strawberry gutting to her feet and heading towards the kitchen.

"Hey what's good brah" greated Season sliding into the dinner room all smoothly.

"It's done" Congo cheesed, dapping Season up.

"Stupid mother fucker think he was going to stop fucking with the bad guy, cause of another nigga hating, bad choice, Now look at me, I own your shoes" Season silly ass was talking to New York

Black, dope, money and jewelry as if the nigga could hear every world personally.

Congo just stated at his boy until he was done.

being on top of the world. Season had more personality then a mother fucker.

CHAPTER 21

Gutta: BBL

Shit was going good for Gutta in the game. He finally got his hands on that Cadillac and dropped $15 stacks into it. He had three fly ass plush out three apartments to house his ho's in. Gutta had Fat cat who was a little over two months pregnant nine times out of ten with his seed. A nigga name yell boy Marko thought it was his too, so Gutta knew she was out creeping since they wasn't a official couple.

They pulled up on the track it was a Friday night, Congo was in his crown Vic behind them and Season was pushing God only knew who slime green lambo taking up the rear. Bird was finally on the sense and was really ready to give Gutta his one. A str-8 up head up fight Right on the track. Bird was cleaned up against the side of his lime with mercy up under his arms.

It seemed to him that every pimp and maggot ass ho was on the track waiting to see the show down between himself and Gutta. Bird didn't get nervous until the young pimp Jumped at the sporty lace with his short already off. He could see the in tease.

aggressiveness baring off the young pimp.

"Let's do this Vegas pimping!" called out shawty slick pulling out a huge bankroll.

That stopped Gutta dead in his truck "Who you like shawty slick?"

"I gotta go with experience, young in"

"What you betting, I'm covering all bets!" spoke up Season

Bird had ten minutes to prepare himself for the fight while the bets was being placed. It was over two dozen pimps that he came up in the game who sided with him. The fight kicked off in the middle of the street. Bird wished he wasn't on that glass dick after the first three minutes into the fight. He stood 6'7 and use to weight 255 but since the dope now he was down to 192.

Bard was holding his on using every old school fighting trick he could think off to keep Gutta off his ass, but the young pimp like a wild vicious red nose pit-bull. After Gutta whooped Bird ass real good, Congo and Season jumped into rain Kicks on the old pimp. In their eyes the one on one was just out of respect. The stamp out was the eye for an eye issue.

Remy: BBL

She was up in Bentley Blue's face after just catching him at his Mini-Mansion fucking Cherry + Chocolate in the same bed he shared with her.

"You all up in this mother fucker fucking these nasty as ho's while your wife running around the streets looking for your unfaithful ass, and how could you fuck them to shanks in the bed I picked out for us hush?" Raged Remy.

In the room across from his, Shawty Blue and Cake private sex party was loud and clear. The two been dating heavily ever since that bachelor party night and they was almost inseparable. Bentley Blue didn't hesitate to drop $15,000 like it was hot to hit Cherry and Chocolate both at the same time. What started off as a onetime order ended up turning into a once a week habit.

Bentley Blue was standing ass naked in his own halogen manhood as hard as a rock. He had the double doors to his master bedroom closed behind him.

"Don't be coming up in my shit like you own something up in this bitch. I pay the bills to be the top dog up in here, and you tell Hazel to take her crazy ass home when she calls you. I'm doing me so chill before I put the both of your money supple off" He said as he stroked himself to stay hard.

"Don't be threading me boy or else I'd play that same game with your triflen ass" She shot back, half hearted.

"Look baby, just go to my house and chill with Hazel, I'd be in within three hours Remy cut him off.

"No your coming with me right now and I ain't playing with you Bently, so come on."

Bently, Blue shook his head in defect, as he was about, as he was about to stop back into the bedroom.

"And where you think you gang boy?"

"Inside to get my clothes, Remy"

"No you're not, you about to take your naked butt down stairs and wasn't on we. I'd go inside and get your stuff."

Remy wasn't playing with him either she didn't make a move until Bently Blue was out of sight. She went into the bedroom and turned up her nose at the sight of the two females on her bed. Remy tried to go about her business until Cherry slid into the waling in closet with her naked self.

"Bitch can you get out of my way before I snap!" spoke Remy

"You know it's enough money in this niggas pocket for all of us"

"I'm not about to share what's mine, with you ho's"

"Actually its Hazel money we're all spending freely, everybody already know he's not about to leave that ugly bitch for none of our asses. But you do you because you aint gong to be happy until you make sure that's all there or our asses will be scrappy for money again" Cherry told her seriously.

Remy wasn't trying to hear that shit Cherry was talking, smacking her teeth as she push pass the ho. When she got down stars she threw the cloths in Bentley Blue lap.

"You really need to find better taste in your Ho's" She told him.

Bentley Blue didn't feel like talking or better yet argue about the ho's b was fucking. He was more of the les pissed because he couldn't finish. But he knew Remy had to much dirt on him, and she already be putting up with a lot of his bull shit.

CHAPTER 22

Big T: BBL

Big T have been going back and forth with Peaches all day about him getting out the streets. He couldn't wait for Congo to pull up, they had to make their usual trip to Florida. The 305 boys needed some more toys.

"T I know you hear he talking to you?"

"Peaches you need to stop listen to Coco; I done told you I'm get out when it's time or I'm ready."

"Terry we have more than enough money to start up a small business or true cold invest in something."

"Hell you better invest in me I'm of show money and you know that" Big T stated as he answered his ringing cell phone.

Peaches stood there with her arms folded as she waited for Big T to get off the phone with whoever Big T hung up. The phone and placed it in his pocket, And before Peaches could get a word out, Big T told her that he had to go Congo was out front. He grabbed his load duffle bag and hurried out the door.

"Come on bruh we need to hit the road"

"Nigga I been Ready to get out that house peaches nigga me again about getting out the street" stated Big T as he placed the bag in the trunk next to Congo's bag.

Big T climbed inside the car and Congo drove off ASAP. Congo turned to Big T and told him that Coco being at him for the last few days about the same thing. Congo jumped on the express way and headed to Daytona.

Season: BBL

With New York Black out the picture Season was climbing up the latter pretty fast. Thanks to the help of Congo and Big T. Everything was going good to the point that Season want to put some niggas on up until him.

"Aye yo Gutta!"

"What's up bruh?"

"Aye check this out and I need str-8 up answer on what you think"

"Okay, That want be hard you know we keep it 100 all the times."

"Look, I want to get an Ice-cream truck and sale weed out of it."

"Nigga is you high right now?"

"Nah, for real bruh you know how Big worm did on Friday, I want to do it like that but have me two young niggas working it while I handle my business as usual"

"It's not a bad idea but are you sure it will work?"

"Yeah I know it will, My partner Zay had one a while back but he had to much going on with his it was all tricked out."

"Zay...Zay, why do that name sound familiar?"

"Zay from the projects"

"Oh you talking about Isaiah, Man that wild and crazy ass nigga will try or do anything. But I hear he was up right now."

"Yeah that nigga do so much ain't no telling, but Congo should have looked up with because they are just a like." Season Joked as he got up to head to his Room, To make Pans for his new hustle on sailing his goods.

Coco: BBL

"Girl I been on Congo for the longest trying to get him to stop running the streets."

"I know, Cause Terry say I'm starting to sound like you."

"Oh girl no he didn't go there."

"Yeah girl, but you know me and my baby been doing this for a long and I ain't trying to run him off."

"Girl you know Big T loves yo ass and he ain't going nowhere, but me on the other hand got a lot to worry about. Congo make me feel complete but I know he love the streets more then me."

"Coco you just got to do what I do, Let him run the streets and make his money while you take care of home."

"Yea but peaches that shit get old and I want kids one day with him."

"It will come but at the same time, you don't want to run him off. And you know what talking to lets me know I need to do something special for him when he get back" stated peaches.

"Like what?"

"Girl you better use your imagination, cause I'm give my baby some of this good kitty cat tonight, with a little extra."

"Eww peaches TMT."

"Girl stop acting like you aint letting Congo get all up in that."

"I'm not about to have this conversation with you I got to go" giggled Coco as she hung up the phone.

Congo: BBL

"What's good ATC, you on the road late today aint cha?"

"Yea just a little behind Schedule, but I'm here to do business as usual"

"Ok that's what's up so what you got for me this time?"

"Well this time is a little different got more Rifles them hand guns but here it is, we got a Glock 40, Glock 9, Beretta M9, Colt 1911, PS 90, M149 saw, Tommy gun, Starmegar 44 and a mark 12-7mag, oh yes we got a stinger missile but that's extra."

"How much extra?"

"Just two bands that's all"

"Okay but everything else is the same right?" questioned 305

"Yea it the same bruh no extra charge."

305 signal for one of his guys to bring the money and to help him grab the duffle bags out the punk. Congo tossed Big T the money so he could count it before the walked off. Big T sat in the front seat with a AK 47 between his legs and Tech 9 on his lap while he counted the money. Congo stood out side with his all gold. Desert Eagle up under his shirt and his SK on the back seat just incase they tried something.

"Yo we good right" asked 305

Cong looked down at Big T to see what was the out come. Big T shook his head telling him that it wasn't all there.

"Yo 305, I don't know what type of games you playing but my mans and them side that ain't adding up."

"Yo ATL have yu means to re-count it cause I don't play about no money."

Congo 305 asked Congo if they could get their hands on some vests or grenades. "I'll see what I can do because I need a few myself."

Congo stated as he look back through the window at Bigt to check the status. Big T shook his head no then motion 2000.

"He say you short $2,000 homie"

"Ain't no way I counted it twice myself before I put it in the bag."

"Wel somebody wrong and I need my money or guns back which one my nigga" Congo expressed as he clutched on the pistol under his shirt.

"So you city nigga what to take it there, huh?"

"We about business don't have time for bullshit."

305 partner peeked the move and tried to draw down but Big T beat him to it Congo up his strip on 305 and told him to make his homie drop the guy. Standing there at a stand steal, they finally lower the guns and Big T throw the money on the hood of the car.

"There it is count it yourself" Big T shouted 305 grabbed the bag and went to continue it.

"It's 12000 just like last time"

"Yeah but it's not supposed to be 12,000 it's supposed to be 14, because you got the stinger missile."

"Yeah you right that my fult but it's no pressure, yo troll grab that out of the car and bring it to ATL."

Trill ran back to the car grab a small brow envelope and gave it to Congo. He opened it up and quickly breezed through it.

"It's good" stated Congo"

"I told you, I always do good business."

Congo dapped 30s up and jumped I the car. He wasted no time getting on the road.

Gutta: BBL

Gutta had done became one of the most well respected pimps in the game at the time. After the show down with Bird everybody from young to old knew Gutta was about his issue. And he finally tricked Ice-cream on the track and she was bring in more money than all his other hoes. He knew she had a gold mind between her legs, and it was really show off. And Apple bottom and Baby phat was holding their own, now what they were under Gutta's pimping laws, and rules. Gutta sat on the block over in his new Cadillac, Collecting his money. H even had other pimps paying him to watch there ho's while they handle other business or just wanted to fuck off. And they all knew Gutta services wasn't cheap. He let that be known a while back when he had got into it with that fake ass pimp Truelove.

The track was live and bumping. Gutta sat in his Cadillac counting his money and thinking about how he need to treat his girls for make all this good money. It was getting super late and Gutta was getting sleepy, so he begun Rounding all of his ho's up to let them know it was over with for the night.

"Where the hell is Tweety and J-10?"

"Here comes J-10 now daddy" said Ice-cream.

"Ok well all we need now is Tweety and we gone call it a night."

"So what yall want to stay out one more hour?" questioned Gutta

All at once that shouted "Yes" and Apple bottom even took it a step farther and told him it was more money for him. Gutta went to smiling at the thought of this ho's loved saling that pussy for him.

CHAPTER 23

Congo: BBL

Somewhere down the Road Congo made a wrong turn, and ended up by some apartments that looked close but had cars outside of them. His and Big T turned out the lights as they turned around not trying to get caught up in to anything. But as they were turning around Big T spotted four dread head going inside one apartment until. And all of them was carrying some type of duffle bag.

"Yo Congo Slow down for a minute we might be on to something."

"Shidd what you see?"

"A come up that's what, four dread head just want inside one of the apartment units and all of them had duffle bags."

Congo stopped the car and backed up then parked it right next to a Miami Dolphin painted Donk. Congo turned the car off and grabbed the SK off the back seat. Him and Big T checked all of their clips because they didn't know what might happen. They scan the area for cameras before they got out the car. Trying to stay under the radar, they both scaled the apartment building like they were in the Army of Navy.

The Closer they got the louder the music got. Congo Reached for the door knob while standing on th side to block any ones view of seeing him. As he twisted the knob he felt some one on the other side twisting as well. His eyes got buck as he signal with his head to Big T to get Ready. Congo pushed the door in hard with a lot of force.

Making the door hit whoever it was on the other side in the head. The guy stumbled back and Big T and Congo rushed in. Big T swept the guy feet right from under him making him hit the floor. Congo stayed on point aiming down the hall.

"Are my nigga we can do this the easy way or the hard way, it don't matter to me. Where its at?" Big T aggressively spoke.

"Man I'm just a runner I don't know nothing."

"Ok then Mr. Runner, which one of these is the trap spot?"

"Man you know I can't tell you that they will kill me."

"Don't worry you are already dead."

Big T put one dead in the middle of his eyes. Congo turned and smiled then said "I See what type of party this gone be, so let's see who gone get the most kills."

"So what you saying lil bruh you want to make a small bet."

"We can that will make it funnier."

"Bet how much me betting."

"Just a cool stack."

"Say no more let's get it."

They followed the sound of the loud music that was baring through the walls. But the whole time Congo started getting a feeling that it wasn't gonna go the way they thought. Two guys and chick walked out the door and the music was loud and clear. They knew they found their mark. Congo and Big T unload a few shots taking down one guy and the chick. The other dude made his way back inside with just a glaze.

They ran a few doors down till they made to the apartment door.

"Bruh you want to wait until they come out or you want to go in" asked Big T.

"Bitch we got to go in because they might call somebody to ambush us from out here."

"Yea you right so on the count of three we kick the door then fall back."

"Ok ready....1......2......3"

They both kick the door as hard as they could and it came flying open. Big T and Congo both jumped to the side and hugged the wall, waiting for any type of movement. They just didn't know all of whoever that was in that apartment was waiting on the same thing. Congo stuck the SK around the wall and gun fire was all he heard.

Him and Big T hit the floor crawling on their backs as they kept aim at the front door. Crawling for enough away from the door they got up and ran. And before they could make it to the unit door it opened. Big T and Congo did hesitate to open fire. As soon as the body fell Congo and Big T got back to back to porch themselves. Niggas was coming from every which of way like ants.

"Are Bruh its too many of these fools and if we leave out the apartment unit, we will be out in the open. So we will become better targets for them, so we have to go for what we came for."

"Hell we don't even know what's in this bitch but that sound about right Congo. So let's make it fast in whatever it is we gone do."

"Kill or be kill, you know how we play."

"Yea and I ain't dying today."

Congo and Big T both scooped up M-16s off two dead guys and hung then over their shoulders. Then took off running back to the apartment door. Once then got there they just opened up fire into the apartment, and waited for a few second to see if they were going shoot back. It was strange because nobody shot back. So they ran inside and noticed that the whole.

apartment was gutted out, and sat up for them to codk crack and everything else.

"Boy we hit the jackpot if we can make it out alive" Congo said.

"Man lil bruh we don't have a choice but to make it out."

They searched the unit spotting all of the security cameras, the safe that was left cracked with all the money.

"Deugs and money is all we needed" spoke Big T

"Are we found everything but something feel right bruh, I know we didn't kill all them niggas it was to many."

"Hell we did something cause they ain't here right now so let get what...

Bullets started flying inside the apartment unit.

"Nigga I told you" Congo shouted as he as he returned fire.

"Look bruh stay and put as much money as you can into this duffle bag I'm boot to go make a diversion."

"Ok but be safe and if it get to heated call for me"

"Gotcha"

Big T ducked down and ran out the room, whole Congo quickly filled the bag up. All of the money was wrapped in plastic like it just come out of the bank vault. So it made it easy for Congo to get. Bullets had done stop flying in the room but it continue elsewhere. Congo dragged the big duffle bag out of the room then ran back in and let out a few shots. "That should buy my nigga some time" Congo thought to himself as he drag the duffle bag full speed down the hall.

"Bruh take over the window so I can get some of this work over here." Big T shorted over the gun shots.

Congo unloaded shots like he was Rambo. And the whole shoot out made him feel like he was in the call of duty game but the only different was this shit was real. He looked back to make Big T was alright and all he saw was that big nigga stuffing two duffle bag at the same time. Congo couldn't do nothing but smile and start back shooting.

"Yo Congo this is about good as it gets bruh, now we got to find a way out."

Congo stop shooting because he not only heard what Big T said but he was out of bullets. The SK and M-16 was out the only thing he had left was the Desert Eagle. They both grabbed a dead body and pulled it to the window. Then found three rifles and stuck two out the window with the dead body hand strapped to them as the fired. They gave Big T and Congo time to exit out the back window were the safe was at.

"Damn nigga if I know we were coming back out this way I would have left the money back here" Congo stated.

Big T had both duffle bags full of work strip around his shoulder he could barely move like he wanted to. Congo bag wasn't that heavy but it was heavy enough. They creaked all the way back to the Crown Vic and slowly pupped the trunk and loaded it. As Big T came around to the passenger seat he ripped his shirt, and stuck it in the gas tank of the Miami Dolphin painted Donk and lite it.

Congo waited before he started up the car until the shirt got small enough to explode as they pulled off. As the car went up in flames, Congo was fishtailing it down the road. They got about a half a mile down the street and seen a fleet load of black on black everything, headed pass them going to the apartments. Congo smashed the gas and you could hear the super turbo charger kick in.

He made his way back to 95 and headed home.

CHAPTER 24

Gutta: BBL

The next morning Gutta had all of his ho's at Lenox mall. He was giving them A day of luxury. Letting them get full body massages, shopping, hair and nails done, which was something he did anyways for them. But it was just the fact of how he was letting things Run today.

"Daddy thank you for all of this." Tiny said seductively

"Yall earn it but we are nowhere near finished" Gutta stated

All of the girls eyes got buck in surprise of Gutta's statement. It had been hours pass and Gutta was ready to move on to the next event. They all loaded up, 3 car Cadillac trucks deep.

Season: BBL

Season was putting his plan together with his Ice-cream truck. He had already had the truck, but just needed everything to go in it. He also was trying to remember how Zay was sailing his out of his truck. He wanted to call to get no tis or pointer.

"Baby what are you doing with an Ice-cream truck."

"This is my side business I'm serving nothing but good Ice-cream and snacks throughout the city."

"Boy you are crazy but I'm glad to see you leaving the dope game alone."

"Who said I was doing such a thing the game has been too good to me for me to stop now."

"You, Gutta and Congo are too much, but I got to give it to ya'll, stick together no matter what. And yall make it happen some kind of way."

"Shawty you show enough watching us giant you. You sure you ain't the Feds, APD or DEA" Season teased

"Boy whatever! Look I'm about to go, I have to be at the club early tonight."

"Alight big head call me later." Joked Season

Kiwi rolled her eye and smiled before she walked off.

Congo: BBL

Congo and Big T both had done passed out in front of Big T's apartment. And of it wasn't Peaches They would still be in the car. Congo and Big T both had done got shot and had more than one bullet graze would on them. But at the time their adrenaline was getting that money and dope back to Atlanta.

Peaches had done stitched them up and removed the bullet they each had stuck in them. Congo woke up to the sound of Coco crying.

He looked around then asked "Peaches where Big T at?" And before she could say anything Big T coming running down stairs yelling for Congo.

"Damn yall niggas act like yall go together, Me and my sister don't get no hey how ya'll doing or thanks for patching us up."

"Thank you Peaches but you know that's my dawg and we just been through hell" Congo said with a little sense of humor.

"Yea bae thanks and I guess paying for you to go to med school paid off after all."

"Yea I guess it did but that don't mean yall can just Run around and get all shot up. Me and Coco was crying all night about yall two fools."

Congo looked at Big T and he already knew what was on Congo's mind. "Aye peaches take Coco up stairs while me and Congo handle this business" Big T said as him and Congo headed to the front door. It was time to count up and see what all they had to work with. They brought the duffle bags in and sat them on the floor, and went to work.

An hour and a half later Big T and Congo was happy as hell. They were used to play with thousands but now they were playing with millions. And it was more to come with all of the dope they had.

They each came out on top with 25 million and 25 bricks of Coke and 25 bricks of heroin. Congo couldn't stop cheesing. He loaded his bag up and called Coco down stairs.

He had in his mind that he was about to fuck the dog shit out of her, and try to put a little Congo je in hr.

"Come on Coco lets go we got some business of our own to take care of."

"I like the way that sound daddy." Coco said in a low sexy voice.

Congo gripped the duffle bag tight as he walked to the car. He threw the bag on the back seat then open up the passenger door as he shout the back door. "Umm… I think you might need to follow me in your car baby."

"Why what's wrong with your?" question Coco

"It's blood everywhere in where and I don't know who seen me get out of here last night with them bags."

"Yea you right I'll just meet you over there.

Congo ran back to Big T's door and grabbed a few bullets to put in his Desert Eagle. It was too much money for him to be riding around without no protection. Him and Coco hit the road with Coco leading the way.

Hot: BBL

"Aye Q aint that, nigga Congo' Crown Vic sitting at the red light."

"Yeap that's his shit, now is your time bruh. But how are we going to get him?"

"Don't worry I got it all token care of."

The light turned green and Congo drove off, but before he cross through the inter section, Hot Clipped the tail end of the Crown Viz. Sanding Congo into to a full 360º.

Coco: BBL

"Oh my God, my baby!" Coco scream as the pulled over to the side of the street. As she got out the car she saw two guys standing at Congo's car but neither one of them was Congo. She started walking over but she forgot her phone so she turned around to get it.

Congo: BBL

"Damn they done fuck up my ride, I hope they know they gonna have to pay me for this shit. And where the hell is my phone." Congo thought to himself as he picked his phone off the floor of his Crown Vic. Hearing two niggas outside of his window talking shit he slowly grab his pistol from in between the crack of the seats. Then raised his head up slowly.

Hot: BBL

"Yea pussy nigga I finally caught up with your ass. You done fucked my life up for the last time."

"That's right tell 'em Hot" co-signed Q

"Nigga you been fucking my baby Momma, and I know hat was you who robbed me and best me up that night. And now you thank you the only one that can ride good and get to the money, huh?" Hot went on about Congo fucking him over.

"Man my nigga what you want to hot, cause all that talking ain't gone fix shit and it damn she aint gone fix car you done fucked up" Congo replied aggressively.

"Now I got something even better" Smiled hot

He pulled a glock 9 of his hip.

Congo: BBL

Congo peeped the move before Hot could fully come off his hip with his pistol. And unloaded a few shots out of the car window, Hitting Hot and Q. He know for sure he caught hot in the chest at least once and wasn't quite sure where he hit Q but he seen Hot hit the ground.

Coco: BBL

Coco stopped in mid stride and started screaming dropping her phone and all. She a body falls to the ground and the other guy take off running. Yet alone Congo jumping out the car and shooting the guy in his back two time and one in the neck. Before he climbed back in the car and hauled ass. She couldn't believe her eyes. Coco didn't know Congo was so gangsta, it made her have tingling sensation that she never felt or had before. Coco jumped in her car and followed behind Congo.

Congo: BBL

"Pick up the phone Coco Damn" Congo stressed

"What the hell Congo are you crazy?"

"Yea I might be but look I need to put this stuff in your car and I need for you to follow me to the custom body."

"Ok I'm bere with you baby whatever you need."

Congo pulled over about two blocks down and put the duffle bag in Coco's trunk. He wasted no time getting back to his car and head to the custom paint and body shop.

"Aye man I got Crown Vic I need you to fix rear and paint it a smoke gray, how long will that take?" Congo asked

"Well it depend on how bad the rear is messed up."

"Ok well just hook me up and I'll be back."

"Wait you got to put down a down payment."

Congo reached in his pocket and pull out the small knot of money, that he took of Hot before he got back in the car. "Here's your payment and my number call me as soon its ready" Congo replied before walking off. Congo forgot all about the blood him and Big T left everywhere. But at the same he wasn't worried about it because the body shop was known for flipping stolen cars.

CHAPTER 25

Two years later the whole crew was eating better than they ever had. They were plugged in with any and everybody that had sometime going. They had done built a name for themselves and no matter what state they went to they was shown love.

Gutta had done bought a mini mansion to house all of his was Hugh Healthier. Gutta had about 6 kids.

Season was moving move dope then a little bit. He had 3 Ice-cream for the summer and 4 food trucks for year around. Bentley blue and all the other dealers had to hop with him. He balled like he was Big Meetcha but on a guitar level. Him and Kiui was steal going strong even thou he did his thong on the low.

Gongo was still terrorizing the streets. He and Big T got plugged in with the Cartel. And they were robbing folks for the Cartel and bringing them back half the product and keeping all the money. Coco and peaches was still sticking by their side and they both had babies by them.

And the hustle Continues…….

Printed in the United States
by Baker & Taylor Publisher Services